G K Chesterton was born in London in 1874 and was educated at St Paul's School. He became a journalist and began writing for *The Speaker* with his friend Hilaire Belloc. His first novel, *The Napoleon of Notting Hill,* was published in 1904. In this book Chesterton developed his political attitudes in which he attacked socialism, big business and technology and showed how they become the enemies of freedom and justice. These were themes which were to run through his other works.

Chesterton converted to Catholicism in 1922. He explored his belief in his many religious essays and books. The best known is *Orthodoxy,* his personal spiritual odyssey.

His output was prolific. He wrote a great variety of books from biographies on Shaw and Dickens to literary criticism. He also produced poetry and many volumes of political, social and religious essays. His style is marked by vigour, puns, paradoxes and a great intelligence and personal modesty.

Chesterton is perhaps best known for his Father Brown stories. Father Brown is a modest Catholic priest who uses careful psychology to put himself in the place of the criminal in order to solve the crime.

Chesterton died in 1936.

30

GENERAL FICTION:

THE BALL AND THE CROSS
THE MAN WHO KNEW TOO MUCH
THE MAN WHO WAS THURSDAY
MANALIVE
THE NAPOLEON OF NOTTING HILL
THE PARADOXES OF MR POND
THE RETURN OF DON QUIXOTE
TALES OF THE LONG BOW

FATHER BROWN SERIES:

THE INNOCENCE OF FATHER BROWN
THE WISDOM OF FATHER BROWN
THE INCREDULITY OF FATHER BROWN
THE SECRET OF FATHER BROWN
THE SCANDAL OF FATHER BROWN

BIOGRAPHY:

ST THOMAS AQUINAS
ST FRANCIS OF ASSISI
AUTOBIOGRAPHY
WILLIAM BLAKE
ROBERT BROWNING
CHAUCER
WILLIAM COBBETT
CHARLES DICKENS
GEORGE BERNARD SHAW
ROBERT LOUIS STEVENSON

OTHER WORKS:

THE BALLAD OF THE WHITE HORSE
CRITICISMS AND APPRECIATIONS OF THE WORKS OF CHARLES DICKENS
HERETICS
ORTHODOXY
THE VICTORIAN AGE IN LITERATURE

G K CHESTERTON

The Poet and the Lunatics

EPISODES IN THE LIFE OF GABRIEL GALE

HOUSE OF
STRATUS

This edition published in 2001 by House of Stratus, an imprint of
Stratus Books Ltd., Lisandra House, Fore Street,
Looe, Cornwall, PL13 1AD, U.K.

www.houseofstratus.com

Printed and bound by CPI Group (UK) Ltd, Croydon, CR0 4YY

A catalogue record for this book is available from the British Library
and the Library of Congress.

ISBN 0-7551-0020-4

Contents

I

The Fantastic Friends

The inn called the Rising Sun had an exterior rather suggesting the title of the Setting Sun. It stood in a narrow triangle of garden, more grey than green, with broken-down hedges mingling with the melancholy reeds of a river; with a few dark and dank arbours, of which the roofs and the seats had alike collapsed; and a dingy dried-up fountain, with a weather-stained water-nymph and no water. The house itself seemed rather devoured by ivy than decorated with it; as if its old bones of brown brick were slowly broken by the dragon coils of that gigantic parasite. On the other side it looked on a lonely road leading across the hills down to a ford across the river; now largely disused since the building of a bridge lower down. Outside the door was a wooden bench and table, and above it a wooden sign, much darkened, with the gold of the sun's disc faded to a brown; and under the sign stood the innkeeper, gazing gloomily up the road. His hair was black and flat, and his face, of a congested purple, had all the sombreness, if not all the beauty, of sunset.

The only person in the place who exhibited any liveliness was the person who was leaving it. He was the first and last customer for many months; a solitary swallow who had conspicuously failed to make a summer; and the swallow was now flitting. He was a medical man on a holiday; young, and of an agreeable ugliness, with a humorous hatchet face and red hair; and the cat-like activity of his movements contrasted with the stagnant inertia of the inn by the ford. He was strapping up his own bag on the table under the sign; and neither his host, who stood a yard off, nor the single servant, who moved heavily and obscurely within, offered to help him; possibly through sulkiness, possibly merely through dreaminess and disuse.

The long silence, idle or busy, was broken for the first time by two sharp and explosive sounds. The first was the abrupt bursting of the strap which the doctor was tightening round the bag on the table; and the second was the loud and cheerful "Damn!" which was his comment upon it.

"Here's a pretty go," observed the medical gentleman, who went by the name of Garth; "I shall have to tie it up with something. Have you got a cord or a rope or anything?"

The melancholy innkeeper turned very slowly and went indoors, coming out presently with a length of dusty rope in a loop like a halter, probably for tethering a donkey or a calf.

"That's all I've got," he said; "I'm pretty well at the end of my own tether anyhow."

"You seem a bit depressed," observed Dr Garth; "you probably want a tonic. Perhaps this medicine chest burst open to give you one."

"Prussic acid is the kind of tonic I feel inclined for," answered the landlord of the Rising Sun.

"I never recommend it," observed the doctor cheerfully. "It's very pleasant at the moment, no doubt; but I never feel I can guarantee a complete recovery afterwards. But you certainly seem down in the mouth; you didn't even brighten up when I indulged in such an eccentricity as paying my bill."

"Much obliged to you, sir," observed the other gruffly, "but it would want a lot more bills to keep this rotten old show from going to pot. It was a good business once, when the right-of-way was open beyond the river, and everybody used this ford. But the last squire shut up the path somehow; and now everything goes by the new bridge a mile away. Nobody comes this way; and, saving your presence, I don't know why anybody should."

"Well, they say the new squire is nearly bankrupt himself," observed Dr Garth. "So history brings its revenges. Westermaine's his name, isn't it? I'm told there's a brother and sister living in the big house over there, with precious little to live on. I suppose the whole countryside's rather gone downhill. But you're wrong about nobody coming here," he added suddenly, "for there are two men coming over the hill now."

The road ran across the valley at right angles to the river; beyond the ford the forgotten right-of-way could be traced more faintly up the slope to where the ruined gate that marked Westermaine Abbey stood dark against clouds of a pallor that was faintly lurid, as with a hint of storm. But on the other side of the valley the sky was clear; and the early afternoon seemed as bright and brisk as morning. And on this side, where the white road curved over the hill, two figures were advancing, which seemed, even when they were hardly more than dots in the distance, to be markedly dissimilar.

As they came nearer to the inn, the contrast increased, and was accentuated by the very fact of their air of mutual familiarity; as if they were almost walking arm in arm. One was comparatively short and very sturdy; the other unusually tall and slender. They were both fair; but the blond hair of the shorter man was neatly parted and smoothly plastered down; while that of the other stood up in erratic wisps and tufts that looked fantastic. The shorter man had a full square face sharpened by a very pointed nose, and a pair of bright, bird-like eyes, that made it look like a small beak. There was something of the cock sparrow about him; and, indeed, he seemed more of a town bird than a country bird. His clothes were as neat and commonplace as a clerk's; and he carried a business-like little bag as if he was going up to the City; while his tall companion had bundled on his back a loose knapsack, and what was evidently the paraphernalia of a painter. He had a long, slightly cadaverous face, with absentminded eyes; but the chin beneath jutted forward, almost as if it had formed an unconscious resolution of its own, of which the blank blue eyes were still unaware. They were both young; and they both walked without hats, probably through the heat of walking; for the one held a hard straw hat in his hand, and the other had a loose grey felt stuffed anyhow into his knapsack.

They came to a halt before the inn; and the shorter man said jovially to his companion, "Here's a field for your efforts, anyhow."

Then he called out with breezy civility to the innkeeper, asking him to bring out two pots of ale; and when that gloomy character had disappeared into his gloomy place of entertainment, he turned to the doctor with the same radiant loquacity:

"My friend's a painter," he explained, "but rather a special sort of painter. You might call him a house-painter; but he's not quite what most people mean by one. It may surprise you, sir, but he's an RA, and not the stuffy sort that sometimes suggests, either. One of the first among the young geniuses, and exhibits at all their cranky galleries. But his whole aim and glory in life is to go about repainting inn-signs. There; you don't meet a genius with that little fancy every day. What's the name of this pub?"

And he stood on tip-toe, craning and peering at the blackened sign with an extraordinary contained vivacity in his curiosity.

"The Rising Sun," he commented, turning eagerly again to his silent friend. "That's what you would call an omen, after what you were saying this morning about reviving the real inns. My friend is very poetical; and he said it would make a sunrise all over England."

"Well, they say the sun never sets on the British Empire," observed the doctor, with a laugh.

4

"I don't feel it about the Empire so much," said the painter simply, breaking his silence like one spontaneously thinking aloud. "After all, one doesn't fancy an English inn on the top of Mount Everest, or somewhere on the Suez Canal. But one's life would be well spent in waking up the dead inns of England and making them English and Christian again. If I could do it, I would do nothing else till I die."

"Of course you can do it," replied his travelling companion. "A picture by an artist like you, and hung outside a public-house, makes it fashionable for miles round."

"Is it really true, then," inquired Dr Garth, "that you employ all your serious powers on subjects like public-house signs?"

"What finer subjects are there, even as subjects?" asked the painter; he was now evidently full of his favourite subject, and he was one of those who are either abstractedly silent or ardently argumentative. "Is it more dignified to paint an Academy portrait of some snobbish mayor in a gold chain, or some swindling millionaire's wife in a diamond tiara, than to paint the heads of great English admirals, to be toasted in good ale? Is it better to paint some nepotistical old noodle wearing his George and Garter than to paint St George himself in the very act of killing the Dragon? I've repainted six old signs of St George and the Dragon, or even the Dragon without St George; a sign called the Green Dragon is usually very suggestive to anybody with a little imagination; you can make him a sort of spirit and terror of tropical forests. Even a Blue Boar is suggestive; something nocturnal with stars like the Great Bear; like that dim monstrous boar that stood for chaos and old night in the Celtic mythology."

And he reached for his pewter pot, and applied himself to it with absorption.

"He's a poet as well as a painter, you know," explained the smaller man, still regarding his companion with an absurd air of proprietorship, as if he himself were the keeper and showman of some singular wild animal; "you've probably heard of the poems of Gabriel Gale, illustrated by himself? I can get you a copy if you are interested in these things. I'm his agent and business man; my name's Hurrel – James Hurrel. People laugh at us and call us the Heavenly Twins, because we're inseparable, and I never let him out of my sight. Have to look after him – eccentricities of genius, you know."

The painter took his face off the pewter pot, a face fiery with controversy.

"Genius oughtn't to be eccentric!" he cried in some excitement. "Genius ought to be centric. It ought to be in the core of the cosmos, not on the revolving edges. People seem to think it a compliment to accuse one of being an outsider, and to talk about the eccentricities of genius. What would they think, if I said I only wish to God I had the centricities of genius?"

"I fear they would think it was the beer," replied Dr Garth, "that had slightly confused your polysyllables. Well, it may be a romantic idea to revive the old signs, as you say. Romance is not much in my line."

Mr Hurrel, the agent, cut in sharply, and even eagerly. "But it isn't only a romantic idea," he explained; "it's a real, practical idea, too. I'm a business man, and you may believe me it's really a business proposition. Not only for us, but for the other people too – for the innkeepers and the villagers and the squires, and everybody. Why, look at this broken-down ale-house they call the Rising Sun. If everyone would work together, they could have this empty hole humming like a hive in a year. If the squire would open the old road and let people visit the ruins, if he'd build a bridge here by the inn and hang out a sign painted by Gabriel Gale, you'd have all the cultivated sightseers in Europe stopping here for lunch."

"Hullo!" cried the doctor. "It looks as if they were coming to lunch already. Really, our pessimistic friend inside talked as if this were a ruin in the desert; but I begin to believe it does a trade like the Savoy."

They had all been standing with their backs to the road, looking at the dark tavern under discussion; but even before the doctor began to speak, Gabriel Gale, the painter and poet, had become in some odd fashion conscious of an addition to the company. Perhaps it was because the elongated shadows of a horse and two human figures had for some little time rested on the sunny road beside him. He turned his head over his shoulder, and remained staring at what he saw.

A high dog-cart had drawn up on the other side of the road. The reins were in the gloved hands of a tall, dark young lady, clad in dark blue of the tailor-made type, neat but not particularly new. By her side was a man, perhaps ten years older than herself, but seeming in many ways much more, for his high-featured face was wasted as with sickness, and there was a great anxiety in his large grey eyes.

In the momentary silence the clear voice of the girl came like an echo of the doctor's phrase, saying: "I am sure we can get some lunch here." She slipped lightly to the ground and stood by the horse's head, while her companion descended with a little more hesitation. He was dressed in light tweeds, which seemed somehow slightly incongruous with his invalid air, and he addressed Hurrel with a rather nervous smile.

"I hope you won't regard me as an eavesdropper, sir; but you were not exactly speaking as if you were talking secrets."

Hurrel, indeed, had been talking as if he were a cheap-jack dominating the noise of the fair; and he smiled and answered quite pleasantly:

"I was only saying what anybody might about what a squire might do with a property like this. I don't in the least mind anybody listening who happens to be interested."

"I happen to be a little interested," answered the man in tweeds, "because, as it happens, I am the squire if there are any squires nowadays."

"I sincerely apologise," answered the agent, still smiling; "but, if you will play Haroun Alraschid – "

"Oh, I'm not at all offended," answered the other. "To tell the truth, I'm rather wondering whether you aren't quite right."

Gabriel Gale had been looking at the girl in dark blue rather longer than was quite polite; but painters and absent-minded persons may sometimes be excused in such cases. His friend would probably have infuriated him by calling it one of the eccentricities of genius, but it might have been disputed whether his admiration was entirely eccentric. Lady Diana Westermaine would have made a most satisfactory sign for an inn – a bush worthy of the best wine – or might even have uplifted the lowly estate of an Academy picture, though it was long since her unfortunate family could have easily afforded one. She had hair of a curious dark brown, which in ordinary shades looked black, while the lights in it looked almost red; her dark eyebrows had a touch of temper both in the good and the bad sense; her eyes were even larger and greyer than her brother's, but less filled with mere worry and more with a more spiritual weariness. Gale had the sense that her soul was more hungry than her body. But he had also the thought that people are only hungry because they are healthy. He thought all this in the brief moments before he remembered his manners and turned to consider the other group.

When he had left off looking at her, she began looking at him, but with a somewhat cooler curiosity.

Meanwhile, Mr James Hurrel had been working wonders, not to say miracles. With something more than the tenacity of a tout, with something of the eloquence of the born diplomatist, he had already wound round the squire a web of suggestions and proposals and possibilities. There was really something about him of that imaginative businessman of whom we hear so much and see so little. Affairs which a man like Westermaine could never normally have conceived as being settled except by long lawyers' letters extending over several months, seemed to be arranging themselves before him in several minutes. A new bridge of the most artistic woodwork seemed already to point across the river to the open road; a new and higher class of rents seemed already to be dotting the valley with artistic villages; and a new golden sign of the Rising Sun, with the signature of Gabriel Gale, already blazed above them, a symbol that the sun had risen indeed.

Before they knew where they were the whole company had been bustled in the most friendly fashion through the inn, and set down to a luncheon that was really a committee round the table in the dreary garden beside the river. Hurrel was drawing plans on the wooden table and making calculations on pieces of paper, and reeling off figures and answering objections and growing every moment more restless and radiant. He had one piece of magic for making others believe – the fact that he evidently believed himself; and the squire, who had never met such a person before, had no weapons with which to fight him, even if it had been his interest to do so. Amid all this whirl Lady Diana looked across at Gale, who sat at the opposite corner of the table, somewhat detached and dreamy.

"What do you think of it, Mr Gale?" she said; but Mr Gale's business adviser answered for him, as he answered for everybody and answered for everything.

"Oh, it's no good asking him about business," he cried boisterously. "He's only one of the assets; he brings in all the artistic people. He's a great painter; but we only want a painter to paint. Lord bless you, he won't mind my saying that; he never minds what I say, or what anybody says, for that matter. He doesn't answer a question for about half an hour, as a rule."

Nevertheless, the painter answered the lady's question under the time specified; but all he said was, "I think we ought to consult the innkeeper."

"Oh, very well," cried the resilient Hurrel, leaping up. "I'll do that now, if you like. Back in a minute." And he disappeared again through the dark interior of the inn.

9

"Our friend is very eager," said the squire, smiling; "but, after all, those are the sort of people who get things done. I mean practical things."

The lady was again looking at the painter with a slightly constricted brow; she seemed to be almost sorry for him in his comparative eclipse; but he only smiled and said: "No, I'm no good at practical things."

Almost as he spoke a noise like a sort of cry came through the inn from the road beyond, and Doctor Garth sprang to his feet and stood peering in at the door. The next moment Gale also seemed to rouse himself with a sort of sudden agitation; and the moment after that the others were all following the doctor, who had already started through the house. But when he came to the front door Gale turned for a moment, barring the exit with his tall figure, and said: "Don't let the lady come out."

The squire had already seen over the painter's shoulder a horrible instantaneous image. It was the black figure of a man hanging from the signboard of the Rising Sun.

It was only instantaneous; for the next moment Dr Garth had cut him down, with the assistance of Hurrel, who had presumably uttered the first cry of alarm. The man over whom the doctor was bending was the unfortunate innkeeper; and this was apparently the form in which he took his prussic acid.

After being busy in silence for a few moments, the doctor gave a grunt of relief and said: "He's not dead; in fact he'll be all right presently." Then he said, with a sort of disgust: "Why the devil did I leave that rope there instead of tying up my bag like a tidy professional man? I forgot all about it in all this fuss. Well, Mr Hurrel, the sun nearly rose too late for somebody."

Hurrel and the doctor carried the unfortunate innkeeper into his inn, the latter declaring that the would-be suicide would soon be in a position to be questioned, if questioning was necessary. Gale paced up and down outside in his aimless fashion, frequently frowning at the sign that had served as a gallows (and the table that had probably served as the proverbial stool kicked away) with a frown that seemed not only pained but puzzled.

"This is a most distressing business," said the squire. "Of course, I am a magistrate and all that, but I should hate to have to trouble the poor fellow with the police."

At the sound of the word, Gabriel Gale swung round and said in a loud harsh voice: "Oh, I forgot the police. Of course, he must be locked up in a cell to show him that life is worth living after all, and the world a bright, happy place to live in."

He laughed shortly and frowned heavily, and then after ruminating a moment, said with a certain abruptness:

"Look here, I want to ask you a favour, which may seem an odd one. I want you to let me question this poor chap when he comes to. Give me ten minutes alone with him, and I will promise to cure him of suicidal mania better than a policeman could."

"But why you especially?" asked the doctor, in some natural annoyance.

"Because I am no good at practical things," answered Gale, "and you have got beyond practical things."

There was another silence, and he spoke again with the same strange air of authority.

"What you want is an unpractical man. That is what people always want in the last resort and the worst conditions. What can practical men do here? Waste their practical time in running after the poor fellow and cutting him down from one pub sign after another? Waste their practical lives watching him day and night, to see he doesn't get hold of a rope or a razor? Do you call that practical? You can only forbid him to die. Can you persuade him to live? Believe me, that is where we come in. A man must have his head in the clouds and his wits woolgathering in fairyland, before he can do anything so practical as that."

The group felt a growing bewilderment at his new attitude; it seemed to fill the stage in a strange fashion; nor was it lessened when he actually or apparently fulfilled his undertaking, coming out of the inn twenty minutes afterwards, and cheerfully announcing that the innkeeper would not hang himself again. The next moment he had jumped on to the table under the sign with a large piece of chalk in his hand, and was making sketchy and slashing strokes of design on the brown face of the Rising Sun.

Lady Diana was looking on at the operation with a dark and watchful face. She was of a type more intellectual than the others, and she recognized a real thread of thought running through all that seemed to them transcendental tomfoolery. She had understood the implied irony of his first reference to their host; the moral that had come before the frightful fable. After all, they had certainly been thinking of everything about the inn except the innkeeper. She could see there was an intelligent case, and a practical example, of the occasions when the poet can be more useful than the policeman. But she was conscious also of something baffling about him above and beyond all this; of a disquiet in him with some deeper cause, and something in his eye that belied the new levity of his manner. His draughtsmanship, however, was proceeding in the most dashing and even dazzling fashion, when Lady Diana spoke: "I can't think how you can do it," she said, "on the very place where a man has hung himself like Judas."

"It was the treason, not the despair of Judas, that was really bad," he answered. "I was just thinking of something like that for the picture. I prefer it to Apollo and all that, for a treatment of the sunrise. Look here, you have a big head blocked in with some shadows, in the centre," and he made some bold markings on the sun's disc. "His dark face hidden in his hands like that, but a burst of golden dawn behind like a glory. Red bars of level cloud and a red cock, just there. The greatest of sinners and of saints; his reproach the cock, and his halo the Rising Sun."

The nameless shadow seemed to have fallen from him as he talked and worked; and by an almost symbolic coincidence the strong afternoon sun fell with a strange fullness and splendour upon him and his work, which shone out against a blackening background of clouds continually gathering and darkening on the stormy side of the valley, beyond the ford. Against those masses of sinister purple and indigo, his figure looked like that of some legendary craftsman clad in gold and painting the frescoes of a golden chapel. The impression increased as the head and halo of St Peter grew under his hand; and the lady was of the sort not disinclined to dream herself back in some distant period, about which she did not know too much. She felt herself back among the sacred arts and crafts of the mediaeval world; which were all she knew of the mediaeval world.

Unfortunately, a shadow came between her and the sun in a shape that did not remind her of the mediaeval world. Mr James Hurrel, the agent, his stiff hat a little on one side, jumped on to the same table on which the artist stood, and sat within two yards of him, with dangling legs, and somewhat aggressive cigar. "Always have to keep an eye on him, your ladyship, or he'd be giving 'em away," he called out, and somehow his voice and figure failed to fit in with the picture of pious and primitive craftsmanship.

Diana Westermaine explained to herself lucidly that she had no sort of reason to be angry; but she was exceedingly angry. The conversation of the two had been of no particular intimacy; but its increase to three had a very practical and painful effect of intrusion. She could not imagine why the artist, who was a gentleman, should go about with such a little bounder as his business adviser; and she wanted to hear more about the picture of St Peter, or something interesting. As the agent sat down he had audibly observed something about making room for a little one. If he, at that moment, had been suddenly suspended from the sign, it is doubtful if the lady would have cut him down.

At this moment a much quieter voice said in her ear: "Excuse me, but might I have one word with you?"

She turned and found Dr Garth, with his bag in his hand, evidently about to resume his journey at last.

"I'm going," he said, "and I feel I really ought to tell you something before I go."

He drew her a little way up the road of his departure, and then turned with an abrupt and hurried air of farewell.

"Doctors are often in delicate situations," he said, "and a troublesome sense of duty drives me to saying a rather delicate thing. I tell it to you and not your brother, because I think you have a long way the better nerve of the two. There is something I suspect about those two men who go about painting signs."

From where they stood on the higher ground she could still see the sign itself shining with its new accretion of colours, and the tall, actively moving figure, shining also with sunlight, and from that distance altogether dwarfing the small and dingy figure near his feet. There returned on her still more strongly the vision of a true creator, making pure colours in the innocent morning of the world.

"They are called the Heavenly Twins," went on the doctor, "because they are inseparable. Well, there are many kinds of couples that are inseparable, and many causes for their never separating. But there is one sort that specially concerns me, and I should be sorry to see mixed up with you."

"I haven't the least idea what you mean," replied Lady Diana.

"What about a lunatic and his keeper?" said the doctor, and walked on rapidly along the road, leaving her behind him.

She had the sensation of furiously flinging a suggestion from her, from the top of a high tower to the bottom of an abyss, combined with the sensation that the tower was not high enough nor the abyss deep enough; she even had the novel sensation that there was something weak about her throwing. While the tower of her mind was still rocking with the effort, she was interrupted by her brother, who came hastily, and even excitedly, towards her.

"I've just asked these gentlemen across to our place," he said, "to fix up this business better. And we'd better be starting, for there's a storm beating up, and even the ford sometimes gets pretty dicky. As it is, we shall have to cross two at a time in our own rotten old cart."

It was in a sort of dream that she found herself again untethering the horse and again taking the reins. It was in a dream that she heard the voice that irritated her so much saying, "Heavenly Twins, you know, Heavenly Twins; we mustn't be parted"; and then the voice of the squire replying, "Oh, it'll only be for a minute, anyhow; she'll send Wilson back with the dog-cart at once. There's only room for two at a time, I'm afraid." They stood a little way back in the doorway of the inn as they talked, and Gabriel Gale had just stepped from the table and was standing nearer to the dog-cart.

Then there surged up in her suddenly she knew not what movement of impatience or defiance; and she said in a matter-of-fact tone: "Are you coming first, Mr Gale?"

The face of the artist blanched as if he were blasted with white lightning in the sunlight. He gave one look over his shoulder and then leapt into the seat beside her, and the horse threw up his head and began to move towards the ford. The rain must have already fallen further upstream, for there was already the sensation of water flowing more deeply about the horse's legs; and, though they were only fording a river, she had a hazy sensation of crossing a Rubicon.

Enoch Wilson, the groom, one of the small group left at Westermaine Abbey, died and was gathered to his fathers without having the faintest notion of the determining part which he played in the dark events of that night. And his private life, though, like that of other immortal spirits, of an intense interest, does not in any other point affect this story. It is enough to say that he was rather deaf, and, like many grooms, more sympathetic with the moods of horses than of men. Lady Diana sought him out in the stable, which stood far from the house and near the river, and told him to take the dog-cart back for the rest of the party. She spoke hurriedly and told him to hurry, because the rain would soon make the ford difficult; and her phrases, combined with his own bias, turned his mind chiefly to a consideration of the horse. He drove across under the gathering storm, and as he drew near the dark inn he heard high and excited voices. Mr Hurrel was evidently hot upon his hobby or campaign. The groom got the impression that there was a quarrel; and took a few testy words from his master as meaning that he was not to be disturbed. So the careful Wilson took the horse back across the ford and back into the stable, congratulating himself on having saved the valuable quadruped from the worst inconveniences of what threatened to be a flood. Then he betook himself to his own occupations, leaving a trail of destiny behind him.

Meanwhile Diana Westermaine had left the stable and made her way across the grounds to rejoin the guest who had gone in front of her. As she went up through a lane of hollyhocks and tall plants, she saw the vast flying island or continent of rain cloud, with its volcanic hues and outline, come sailing slowly over the dark, wooded ridge that was the wall of the valley. There was already something faintly lurid about the twilight with which it covered the rich colours of the garden; but higher up the climbing path a strip of lawn was golden in a chance gleam of sunlight, and against it she saw the figure she had come to seek. She recognized it by the light brown clothes that had looked like gold in the evening light, but there was something very extraordinary about the shape as distinct from the colour. He seemed to be waving his arms slowly like branches in a breeze, and she fancied the arms were unnaturally long. For an instant she had the ugly fancy that the figure was deformed; and yet the more unearthly fancy that it had no head. Then the nightmare turned into ordinary nonsense, for the man threw a sort of cartwheel and alighted on his feet laughing. He had actually been standing on his head, or rather on his hands.

"Excuse me," he said, "I often do that. It's a very good thing for a landscape painter to see the landscape upside down. He sees things then as they really are; yes, and that's true in philosophy as well as art." He brooded and then explained explosively.

"It's all very well to talk about being topsy-turvy. But when the angels hang head downwards, we know they come from above. It's only those that come from below that always have their noses in the air."

Despite his hilarious manner, she approached him with a certain subconscious fear; which was not lessened when he lowered his voice and added: "Shall I tell you a secret?"

At the same moment were heard overhead the first heavy movements of the thunder, through which his voice came, perhaps, with an accidental air as of loud whispering.

"The world is upside down. We're all upside down. We're all flies crawling on a ceiling, and it's an everlasting mercy that we don't drop off."

At that instant the twilight turned to a white blaze of lightning; and she was shocked to see that his face was quite serious.

She said with a sort of irritation, "You do say such crazy things," and the next moment her voice was lost in the thronging echoes of the thunder, which seemed to shake everything, shouting the same word again and again – crazy, crazy, crazy. She had unconsciously given a word for the worst thought in her mind.

As yet no rain had fallen on the garden slopes, though the noise of it was already troubling the river beyond. But even had it done so, she herself doubted if the man would have noticed it. Even in more normal moments he seemed to be one who singly pursued a solitary train of thought, and he was still talking, like a man talking to himself, about the rationality of topsy-turvydom.

"We were talking about St Peter," he said; "you remember that he was crucified upside down. I've often fancied his humility was rewarded by seeing in death the beautiful vision of his boyhood. He also saw the landscape as it really is: with the stars like flowers, and the clouds like hills, and all men hanging on the mercy of God."

Then a heavy drop of rain fell on him; and the effect of it was indescribable. It seemed to sting him like a wasp and wake him out of a trance. He started and stared round; and then said in a new and more natural voice:

"My God, where is Hurrel? What are the others doing? Aren't they here yet?"

With an impulse not to be analysed, Diana dashed through the swaying plants to the top of a neighbouring hillock, and looked across the valley to the inn of the Rising Sun. And she saw flowing between them and that place a heavier and wider flood, which in that wild moment looked impassable, like the river of death.

In a strange way it seemed to her a symbol of something greater than the mere grim realism that would have told her, now only too plainly, that she was left alone with a lunatic. Somehow it seemed that the lunacy itself was only a sort of abominable accident and obstacle between her and something that might have been beautiful and a satisfaction of the soul. Another dark river was flowing between her and her own fairyland.

At the same moment Gabriel Gale gave a terrible cry; he also had seen afar off the sundering flood.

"You were right, after all," he said. "You spoke of Judas, when I dared to speak of Peters. I have blasphemed and done the unpardonable sin. I am the traitor now." Then he added in lower and heavier tones: "Yes, I am the man who sold God."

The girl's mind was growing clearer with the cold pain of reality. She had heard that maniacs sometimes accused themselves of the unpardonable sin. Something of her natural courage returned also, and she was ready to do anything, though she did not yet see very clearly what to do. As she was fighting for a solution, the question was settled for her in some degree by her companion himself, who started running down the slope.

"I must get across again if I swim the river," he said. "I ought never to be away from Hurrel like this. I can never tell what will happen next."

She followed his descent, and was rather surprised to see him deflect it to dart towards the stable. Before she knew where she was, he was struggling with the horse and dragging it out into the shafts; and she felt an irrational pleasure in the fact that he had the strength of a man, if it was the strength of a madman. But her own high spirit and self-respect had returned to her, and there rose in her a furious refusal to be a passive spectator of what might well be merely a suicide. After all, however mad he might be, the man was doing the right thing in trying to rejoin his medical attendant; and she would not have the last effort of his sanity frustrated by the antics of his disease.

"I'll drive if we must," she said in a ringing tone. "He'll go better with me."

The sun had set behind the hills opposite, and night was already deepening the darkness of the storm. As the rocking vehicle splashed up to the hub of its wheel in the eddying water, she could only faintly see the long water-rushes streaming with the stream, as if they were indeed the shades of the underworld hovering without hope beside the Styx. But she had no longer need to call it, merely in metaphor, a river of death. Death was driving hard against horse and cart, staggering the insecure foothold of the one, and swaying the human burden of the other; the thunder was about their ears, and on their dreadful path scarce any light but the lightning; and her human companion was a man uttering a monologue, of which she heard snatches, more shocking than the thunder. All the reason and realism in her told her that he might at any moment tear her in pieces. But underneath all such things there was something else contrary and incredible; something in the need and the companionship, and the courage and heroism she was showing; and it was too deep in her dizzy soul for her to know that it was exultation.

The horse almost fell just as they came to the end of the ford, but Gale sprang from the cart and held it, standing knee-deep in water.

In a lull in the noise of the storm she heard for the first time voices from the inn beside the river – voices high, and even shrill, as if the altercation that the groom had heard had risen steadily like the rise of the storm. Then there came what sounded like the crash of a falling chair. Gale dragged the horse to land with the energy of a demon, then dropped the bridle, and set off running towards the inn.

Even as he did so a piercing shriek rose into the night from the doors of that solitary and sinister tavern by the river. It died away in a wailing echo along the reedy banks of the river itself, as if the reeds were indeed the lost spirits by the river of Hades; and the very thunder seemed to have stopped and held its breath to hear it. Then before the thunder moved again came one wide flash of lightning, as wide as an instantaneous daylight, picking out the most minute details of the distance, of the branches and twigs upon the wooded heights, and the clover in the flat fields beside the river. And with the same clarity she saw for an instant something incredible and abominable, and yet not wholly new or unfamiliar – something that returned in the waking world as a detested nightmare will return in sleep. It was the black figure of a man dangling from the painted gallows of the Rising Sun. But it was not the same man.

Diana was convinced for the moment that she herself had gone mad. She could only imagine dully that her own mind had snapped under the strain, and that the dark objects she saw were but dancing dots upon a void. But one of those black dots had certainly seemed to be the figure of her own brother thus lassoed to the beam; and the other black dot, literally a dancing dot, had been the figure of that energetic businessman, Mr James Hurrel. For just then his energy was taking the form of dancing; he was hopping and capering with excitement in front of that frightful signboard.

Darkness followed the flash, and a moment after she heard the great voice of Gale himself, a larger and louder voice than she had imagined him to possess; bellowing through the darkness and the stress of wind. "It's all right – he's quite safe now." Little as she understood of anything yet, she understood with a cold thrill that they had come just in time.

She was still dazed when she staggered somehow through the din and distraction of the tempest into the inn parlour, with a smoky lamp on the table, and the three figures of that frustrated tragedy around it. The squire, her brother, in a sort of collapse of convalescence, sat or lay in an armchair with a stiff dose of brandy in front of him. Gabriel Gale was standing up, like one who had taken command, with a face as white but as hard as marble. He was speaking to the man named Hurrel in low, level, and quiet tones, but with one finger pointed, as when a man speaks to a dog.

"Go over there and sit by the window," he said. "You must keep quite quiet."

The man obeyed, taking a seat at the other end of the room, and looked out of the window at the storm, without hearing or seeking to hear the talk of the others.

"What does it all mean?" asked Diana at last. "I thought you – the truth is Dr Garth gave me a hint that you were only a lunatic and his keeper."

"And so we are, as you see," answered Gale; "but the keeper has behaved far worse than the lunatic."

"But I thought you were the lunatic," she said with simplicity.

"No," he replied; "I am the criminal."

They had drawn nearer to the doorway, and their voices also were covered by the noise of the elements, so that they were almost as much alone as when they stood beyond the river. She remembered the earlier dialogue, and the violent and mysterious language he had used in it; and she said doubtfully: "You said things like that and worse over the other side, and that's what made me think so. I couldn't understand why you should say such wild things against yourself."

"I suppose I do talk rather wildly," he said. "Perhaps you were not so wrong, after all, and I have a streak of sympathy with lunatics – and that's why I can manage them. Anyhow, I happen to be the only person who can manage this particular lunatic. It's a long story, and perhaps I shall tell it some day. This poor fellow once did me a great service, and I feel I can only repay it by looking after him and saving him from the infernal brutality of officials. You see, the truth is they say I have a talent for it – a sort of psychological imagination. I generally know what they're going to do or fancy next. I've known a lot of them, one way or another – religious maniacs who thought they were divine or damned, or what not; and revolutionary maniacs, who believed in dynamite or doing without clothes; or philosophical lunatics, of whom I could tell you some tall stories, too – men who behaved as if they lived in another world and under different stars, as I suppose they did. But of all the maniacs I have tried to manage, the maddest of all maniacs was the man of business."

He smiled rather sourly, and then the tragedy returned to his face as he went on:

"As for your other question, I may have talked wildly against myself, but I didn't talk worse than I deserve. Hadn't I deserted my post, like a traitor? Didn't I leave my wretched friend in the lurch, like a Judas? It's true he'd never broken out like this before; but I was sure in my heart there was one of his antics mixed up with that first affair of the innkeeper. But the innkeeper really was suicidal, and I fancy Hurrel only helped him, so to speak; but it was that that put the damnable notion in his head. I never dreamed he would break out against your brother, or I would – but why do I try to make excuses when there is no excuse? I followed my own will till it went within an inch of murder; and it's I who ought to be hanging from the wooden sign, if hanging weren't too good for me."

"But why – " she began automatically, and then stopped dead, with the sense of a whole new world surging up against her.

"Ah, why," he repeated with a changed voice; "but I think you know why. It is not your fault, but you know why. You know what has often made a sentinel leave his post. You know what brought Troilus out of Troy and perhaps Adam out of Eden. And I have neither the need nor the right to tell you."

She stood looking out into the darkness, and her face wore a singular smile.

"Well, there's the other story you promised to tell some day," she said. "Perhaps you will tell it me if we meet again." And she held out her hand in farewell.

The sinister and fantastic partners had set off again next morning when the sun first shone upon the road; the storm had rolled away along the valley and the birds were singing after the rain. Stranger things yet were to happen before he and she should meet again; but for the moment she had a curious relapse into repose and contemplation. She reminded herself of the words about the world being upside down; and thought it had indeed turned upside down many times in that single night. And she could not analyse the sensation that, in spite of everything, it had come the right side up.

II

THE YELLOW BIRD

Five men had halted at the top of a hill overlooking a valley beautiful enough to be called a vision, but too neglected ever to have been vulgarized by being called a view. They were a sketching club on a walking tour; but when they had come to that place they did no more walking, and, strangely enough, very little sketching. It was as if they had come to some quiet end of the world; that corner of the earth seemed to have a curious effect on them, varying with their various personalities, but acting on all as something arresting and vaguely final. Yet the quality was as nameless as it was unique; there was nothing definably different from twenty other wooded valleys in those western shires upon the marches of Wales. Green slopes dived into a fringe of dark forests that looked black by comparison, but the grey columns of which were mirrored in the curving river like a long winding colonnade. Only a little way along, on one side of the river, the bank was cleared of timber, and formed a platform for old gardens and orchards, in the midst of which stood an old tall house, of a rich brown brick with blue shutters, and rather neglected creepers clinging to it, more like moss to a stone than like flowers to a flower-bed. The roof was flat, with a chimney near the centre of it, from which a thin thread of smoke was drawn up into the sky; the only sign that the house was not wholly deserted. Of the five men who looked down at the landscape, only one had any special reason for looking at the house.

The eldest of the artists, a dark, active, ambitious man in spectacles, destined to be famous afterwards under the name of Luke Walton, was affected by the place in a curious fashion. It seemed to tease him like a fly or something elusive; he could not please himself with a point of view, but was perpetually shifting his camp-stool from place to place, crossing and recrossing the theatre of these events amid the jeers of his companions. The second, a heavy, fair-haired man named Hutton, stared at the scene in a somewhat bovine fashion, made a few lines on a sketching block, and then announced in a loud voice that it was a good place for a picnic, and that he was going to have his lunch. The third painter agreed with him; but as he was said to be a poet as well as a painter, he was expected to show a certain fervour for any opportunities of avoiding work. Indeed, this particular artist, whose name was Gabriel Gale, did not seem disposed even to look at the landscape, far less to paint it; but after taking a bite out of a ham sandwich, and a swig at somebody else's flask of claret, incontinently lay down on his back under a tree and stared up at the twilight of twinkling leaves; some believing him to be asleep, while others more generously supposed him to be composing poetry. The fourth, a smaller and more alert man named Garth, could only be regarded as an honorary member of the artistic group; for he was more interested in science than in art, and carried not a paint-box but a camera. Nevertheless, he was not without an intelligent appreciation of scenery, and he was in the act of fixing up his photographic apparatus so that it covered the angle of the river where stood the neglected garden and the distant house. And at that moment the fifth man, who had not yet moved or spoken, made so abrupt and arresting a gesture that one might say that he struck up the camera, like a gun pointed to kill.

"Don't," he said; "it's bad enough when they try to paint it."

"What's the matter?" asked Garth. "Don't you like that house?"

"I like it too much," said the other, "or rather, I love it too much to like it at all."

The fifth man who spoke was the youngest of the party, but he had already at least some local success and celebrity; partly because he had devoted his talent to the landscape and legends of that countryside, and partly because he came of a family of small squires whose name was historic in those hills. He was tall, with dark brown hair and a long brown face, with a high-bridged nose that looked rather distinguished than handsome; and there was a permanent cloud of consideration on his brow that made him seem much older than his years. He alone of all these men had made no gesture, either of labour or relaxation, on coming to the crest of the hill. While Walton went to and fro, and Hutton started cheerfully on his meal, and Gale flung himself on the couch of leaves to look up into the treetops, this man had stood like a statue looking across the valley to the house, and it was only when Garth pointed his camera that he had even lifted a hand.

Garth turned on him a humorous face, in spite of its hard angular features; for the little scientist was a man of admirable good temper.

"I suppose there's a story about it," he said; "you look as if you were in quite a confidential mood. If you like to tell me, I assure you I can keep a secret. I'm a medical man and have to keep secrets, especially those of the insane. That ought to encourage you. "

The younger man, whose name was John Mallow, continued to gaze moodily across the valley, but there was something about him that suggested that the other had guessed right, and he was about to speak.

"Don't bother about the others," said Garth, "they can't hear; they're too busy doing nothing. Hutton," he called out in much more strident tones, "Gale, are you fellows listening?"

"Yes; I'm listening to the birds," came the half-buried voice of Gale out of his leafy lair.

"Hutton's asleep," observed Garth with satisfaction. "No wonder, after all that lunch. Are you asleep, Gale?"

"Not asleep, but dreaming," answered the other. "If you look up long enough, there isn't any more up or down, but a sort of green, dizzy dream; with birds that might as well be fishes. They're just odd shapes of different colours against the green, brown and grey, and one of them looks quite yellow."

"A yellow hammer, I suppose," remarked Garth.

"It doesn't look like a hammer," said Gale, sleepily; "not such an odd shape as all that."

"Ass!" said Garth briefly. "Did you expect it to look like an auctioneer's hammer? You poets who are so strong about Nature are generally weak in natural history. Well, Mallow," he added, turning to his companion, "you've nothing to fear from them, if you like to talk in an ordinary voice. What about this house of yours?"

"It's not mine," said Mallow. "As a matter of fact, it belongs to an old friend of my mother's, a Mrs Verney, a widow. The place has very much run to seed now, as you see, for the Verneys have got poorer and poorer, and don't know what to do next, which is the beginning of the trouble. But I have passed happier times there than I shall probably ever have again."

"Was Mrs Verney so enchanting a character?" asked his friend softly; "or may I take the liberty of supposing there was a rising generation?"

"Unfortunately for me, it is a very rising generation," replied Mallow. "It rises in a sort of small revolution; and it rises rather above my head." Then, after a silence, he said somewhat abruptly, "Do you believe in lady doctors?"

"I don't believe in any doctors," answered Garth. "I'm one myself."

"Well, it isn't exactly lady doctors, I believe, but it's something of that sort," went on Mallow; "study of psychological science, and so on. Laura has got it very badly, and is helping some Russian psychologist or other."

"Your narrative style is a little sketchy," remarked Dr Garth, "but I suppose I may infer that Laura is a daughter of Mrs Verney, and also that Laura has some logical connexion with the happy days that will not return."

"Suppose it all, and have done with it," replied the young man. "You know what I mean; but the real point is this. Laura has all the new ideas, and has persuaded her mother to come down off the high horse of genteel poverty in all sorts of ways. I don't say she's not right in that; but as it works out there are some curious complications. For one thing, Laura not only earns her own living but earns it in the laboratory of this mysterious Muscovite; and for another, she has bounced her mother into taking a paying guest. And the paying guest is the mysterious Muscovite again, who wants a quiet rest in the country."

"And I suppose, I may take it," said the doctor, "that you feel there is a little too much of the Muscovite in your young life?"

"As a matter of fact, he moved into the house late last night," continued Mallow, "and I suppose that's really why I drifted in this direction this morning, trailing you all at my heels. I said it was a beautiful place, and so it is; but I don't want to paint it, and I don't even want to visit it; but all the same, I had a vague sort of feeling I should like to be somewhere near."

"And, as you couldn't get rid of us, you brought us along," said Garth with a smile. "Well, I think I can understand all that. Do you know anything about this Russian professor?"

"I know nothing whatever against him," answered the other. "He is a very famous man both in science and politics. He escaped from a Siberian prison in the old days, by blowing up the wall with a bomb of his own construction; it's quite an exciting story, and he must at least be a man of courage. He has written a great book called 'The Psychology of Liberty,' I believe; and Laura is very keen on his views. It's rather an indescribable thing altogether; she and I are very fond of each other, and I don't think she mistakes me for a fool, and I don't think I am a fool. But whenever we have met lately it has been literally like a meeting on a high road, when two people are going opposite ways. And I think I know what it is; she is always going outwards, and I am always going inwards. The more I see of the world, and the more men I meet or books I read or questions I answer, the more I come back with increased conviction to those places where I was born or played as a boy, narrowing my circles like a bird going back to a nest. That seems to me the end of all travel, and especially of the widest travel – to get home. But she has another idea in her mind. It's not only that she says that old brown brick house is like a prison, or that the hills are like walls shutting her in; I dare say things do get pretty dull in such a place. There's a theory in it, too, which I suppose she's got from her psychological friend. She says that even in her own valley, and in her own garden, the trees only grow because they radiate outwards, which is only the Latin for branching. She says the very word 'radiant' shows it is the secret of happiness. There is something in it, I suppose; but I radiate inwards, so to speak; that is why I paint all my pictures of this little corner of the world. If I could only paint this valley, I might go on to paint that garden; and, if only I could paint that garden, I might be worthy to paint the creeper under her window."

The sleeping Hutton awoke with an uproarious yawn, and, lifting himself from his bed of leaves, wandered away to where the more industrious Walton had at last settled down to work on the other side of the hill. But the poet Gale still lay gazing at his topsy-turvydom of treetops. And the only reply he would make to a further challenge from Garth was to say heavily, "They've driven the yellow one away."

"Who have driven what away?" demanded Mallow, rather irritably.

"The other birds attacked the yellow one and drove it away," said the poet.

"Regarded it as an undesirable alien, no doubt," said Garth.

"The Yellow Peril," said Gale, and relapsed into his dreams.

Mallow had already resumed his monologue:

"The name of this psychologist is Ivanhov, and he's said to be writing another great book in his country retreat; I believe she is acting as his secretary. It is to embody some mathematical theory about the elimination of limits and – "

"Hullo!" cried Garth. "This moated grange of yours is actually coming to life. Somebody is actually beginning to open a window."

"You haven't been looking at it as I have," answered Mallow quietly. "Just round the angle on the left there's a little window that's been open all the time. That belongs to the little sitting-room out of the spare bedroom. It used to be Laura's room, and still has a lot of her things in it; but I think they give it now to their guests."

"Including, doubtless, their paying guest," observed Garth.

"He's a queer sort of guest. I only hope he's a paying one," returned the other. "That big window where they just opened the shutters is at the end of the long library; all these windows belong to it. I expect they'll stick the philosopher in there if he wants to philosophise."

"The philosopher seems to be philosophical about draughts," observed Dr Garth; "he or somebody else has opened three more windows, and seems to be struggling with another."

Even as he spoke the fifth window burst open, and even from where they stood they could see a creeper that had strayed across it snap and drop with the gesture. It had the look of the snapping of some green chain securing the house like a prison. It had almost the look of the breaking of the seal of a tomb.

For Mallow, against all his prejudices, felt the presence and pressure of that revolutionary ideal which he recognized as his rival. All along the shattered façade of the old brown house the

31

windows were opening one after another like the eyes of an Argus waking from his giant sleep. He was forced to admit to himself that he had never seen the place thus coming to life from within, as a plant unfolds itself. The last three windows were now open to the morning; the long room must already be full of light, to say nothing of air. Garth had spoken of a philosopher enduring draughts; but it seemed more as if a pagan priest had been turned into a temple of the winds. But there was more in that morning vision than the mere accident of a row of windows open when they were commonly closed. The same fancy about unfolding life seemed to fill the whole scene like a new atmosphere. It was as if a fresh air had streamed out of the windows instead of into them. The sun was already fairly high, but it came out of the morning mists above the house with something of the silent explosion of daybreak. The very shapes of the forest trees, spreading themselves like fans, seemed to repeat the original word "radiant," which he had thought of almost as a Latin pun. Sailing over his head, as if sent flying by a sort of centrifugal force, the clouds still carried into the height of noon the colours of sunrise. He felt all the fresh things that he feared coming at him by an irrepressible expansion. Everything seemed to enlarge itself. Even when his eye fell on a stunted gatepost standing alone in the old garden, he could fancy that it swelled as he stared at it.

A sharp exclamation from his friend woke him from his unnatural daydream, which might rather be called, by a contradiction, a white nightmare of light.

"By blazes! he's found another window," cried the doctor; "a window in the roof."

There was, indeed, the gleam of a skylight which caught the sun at an angle as it was forced upwards, and out of the opening emerged the moving figure of a man. Little could be seen of him at that distance, except that he was tall and slim and had yellow hair which looked like gold in the strong sun. He was dressed in some long, light-coloured garment, probably a dressing-gown, and he stretched his long limbs as if with the sleepy exultation of one arisen from sleep.

"Look here!" said Mallow suddenly, an indescribable expression flashing across his face and vanishing; "I'm going to pay a call."

"I rather thought you might," answered Garth. "Do you want to go alone?"

As he spoke he looked round for the rest of the company, but Walton and Hutton were still chatting some distance away on the other side of the hill, and only Gale still lay in the shadow of the thick trees staring up at the birds, as if he had never stirred. Garth called to him by name, but it was only after a silence that Gale spoke. What he said was: "Were you ever an isosceles triangle?"

"Very seldom," replied Garth with restraint. "May I ask what the devil you are talking about?"

"Only something I was thinking about," answered the poet, lifting himself on to one elbow. "I wondered whether it would be a cramping sort of thing to be surrounded by straight lines, and whether being in a circle would be any better. Did anybody ever live in a round prison?"

"Where do you get these cracked notions?" inquired the doctor.

"A little bird told me," Gale said gravely. "Oh, it's quite true."

He had risen to his feet by this time, and came slowly forward to the brow of the hill, looking across at the house by the river. As he looked his dreamy blue eyes seemed to wake up, like the windows opening in the house he gazed at.

"Another bird," he said softly, "like a sparrow on the house tops. And that fits in with it exactly."

There was some suggestion of truth in the phrase, for the strange figure was standing on the very edge of the roof, with space below him and his hands spread out almost as if he wished to fly. But the last sentence, and still more the strange manner in which it was spoken, puzzled the doctor completely.

"Fits in with what?" he asked, rather sharply.

"He's like that yellow bird," said Gale vaguely. "In fact, he is a yellow bird, with that hair and the sun on him. What did you say you thought it was – a yellow hammer?"

"Yellow hammer yourself," retorted Garth; "you're quite as yellow as he is. In fact, with your long legs and straw-coloured hair, you're really rather like him."

Mallow, in his more mystical mood, looked strangely from one to the other, for indeed there was a certain vague similarity between the two tall, fair-haired figures, the one on the house and the other on the hill.

"Perhaps I am rather like him," said Gale quietly. "Perhaps I'm just sufficiently like him to learn not to be like him, so to speak. We may both be birds of a feather, the yellow feather; but we don't flock together, because he likes to flock by himself. And as to being a hammer, yellow or otherwise, well, that also is an allegory."

"I decline to make head or tail of your allegories," said Dr Garth shortly.

"I used to want a hammer to smash things with," continued Gale; "but I've learnt to do something else with a hammer, which is what a hammer is meant for; and every now and then I manage to do it."

"What do you mean by that?" inquired the doctor.

"I can hit the right nail on the head," answered the poet.

It was not, in fact, until later in the day that Mallow paid his call at Mrs Verney's house. Mrs Verney was going up to the neighbouring village for the afternoon; and Mallow had more than one motive for making his attack when the stranger was alone with his secretary. He had a general idea of using his friends to detach or detain the stranger while he himself sought for explanation from the secretary; so he dragged Garth and Gale along with him to Mrs Verney's drawing-room; or rather he would have done so if Gale had been an easy person to drag successfully anywhere. But Gale had a tendency to get detached from any such group, and was always being left behind. Large as he was, he had a way of getting mislaid. His friends forgot him, as they had almost forgotten him when he was lying under the tree. It was not that he was unsociable; on the contrary, he was very fond of his friends and very fond of his opinions, and always delighted to detail the latter to the former. Strangers would have said that he was very fond of the sound of his own voice, but friends who were fond of him knew better. They knew that he had hardly ever heard his own voice, in the sense of listening to it. What made his movements incalculable was that his thinking or talking would start from any small thing that seemed to him a large thing. What are to most men impressions, or half impressions, were to him incidents; and the chief incidents of the day. Many imaginative people know what is meant by saying that certain empty rooms or open doors are suggestive; but he always acted on the suggestion. Most of them understand that there can be something vaguely inviting about a gap in a garden hedge, or the abrupt angle of a path; but he always accepted the invitation. The shape of a hill, or the corner of a house, checked him like a challenge. He wrestled with it seriously till it had given up something of its secret, till he could put something like a name to his nameless fancy; and these things were the active adventures of his life. Hence it was that he would sometimes follow one train of thought for hours, as steadily as a bird winging its way homewards. But it might start anywhere; and hence, in his actual movements, he looked more like a floating tuft of thistledown caught upon any thorn.

On this occasion his friends lost him, or left him behind, as they turned the corner of the house just after passing an old-fashioned bow window looking out on the garden. Inside the window stood a small round table on which was a bowl of goldfish; and Gale stopped abruptly and stared at it as if he had never seen such a thing before. He had often maintained that the main object of a man's life was to see a thing as if he had never seen it before. But in this case the twilight of the little empty room, touched here and there with the late afternoon sunlight, seemed somehow a subtle but suitable background for the thing that he saw. The heart of a dark green sphere was alive with little living flames.

"Why the devil do they call them goldfish?" he asked almost irritably. "They're a much more gorgeous colour than gold; I've never seen it anywhere except in very rare red clouds in a sunset. Gold suggests yellow, and not the best yellow either; not half so good as the clear lemon yellow of that bird I saw today. They're more like copper than gold. And copper is twenty times finer than gold. Why isn't copper the most precious metal, I wonder?"

He paused a moment and then said reflectively: "Would it do, I wonder, when one changed a cheque into gold, to give a man coppers instead, and explain that they have more of the rich tones of sunset?"

His inquiry remained unanswered, for he made it to the empty air. His companions were deficient in his sense of the importance of goldfish, and had gone on impatiently to the main entrance of the house, leaving him lingering by the bowl near the bow window. He continued to look at it for a considerable time, and when at last he turned away, it was not to follow his friends, but to pace the paths of the garden in the deepening and darkening twilight, revolving in his mind some occult romance beginning with a bowl of fish.

Meanwhile, his more practical friends, pursuing the main purpose of the story, had penetrated into the house and found at least some members of the household. There had been many things in the garden or the gateway over which Mallow also might have been disposed to linger if his mood had been merely sentimental; an old swing standing by the corner of the orchard, the angle of a faded tennis lawn, the fork of a pear tree, all of which had stories attached to them. But he was possessed of a passionate curiosity far too practical for sentiment of the merely reminiscent sort; he was resolved to run to earth the mystery of the new man in the old house. He felt that a change had come over everything with the man's mere presence; and wished to know how far that change had gone. He half expected to see those familiar rooms swept bare, or filled with strange furniture where the stranger had passed.

Accident, indeed, gave to their passage through those empty rooms an air of pursuit, as if something were escaping. For, as they passed from an outer room into the long library, the stranger, who was at the other end by the window, emphasized his restless love of the open air by putting one long leg over the low window-sill and stepping out on to the lawn. He had evidently, however, no real desire to avoid them, for he stood there smiling in the sunlight, and uttered some greeting very pleasantly with a slight foreign accent. He was still wearing the long lemon-coloured dressing-gown which, along with his yellow hair, had suggested the comparison of a yellow bird. Under the yellow hair his brow was broad but not high, and the nose was not only long and straight, but came down in a single line from the forehead in the manner that may be seen on many Greek coins and carvings, but which has an unnatural and even sinister symmetry when seen in real life. There was nothing else eccentric or exuberant about him; his manners were casual, but not ungraceful; and nothing contradicted the sunny ease of his situation and demeanour except, perhaps, a slightly strained look in the eyes, which were eager and prominent. Until his acquaintances grew accustomed to it, as a fixed involuntary feature of his face, they occasionally had a sort of shock when catching his quiet face in shadow and realizing that the round eyes were standing out of his head.

The first thing the eyes seemed to encounter was Dr Garth's hand-camera; and, as soon as introductions and salutations had passed, he plunged into talk about photography. He prophesied its extension at the expense of painting, and brushed aside the objection, which even the doctor offered, that painting had the superiority in colour.

"Colour photography will soon be completed," he said hastily; "or rather, it will never be completed, but will always be improved. That is the point of science. You know more or less finally what can be done, well or ill, with a draughtsman's chalk or a sculptor's chisel. But with us the instruments themselves are always changing. That's the real triumph of a telescope – that it is telescopic."

"Well," said Mallow grimly, "I shall wait for one more change in the camera as a scientific instrument before I cut up my old easel for firewood."

"What change is that?" asked the Russian with a kind of eagerness.

"I shall wait till one of those tall cameras walks on its own three legs along a country lane to pick out the view it likes best."

"Even something like that may be more possible than you think," replied the other. "In these days when a man has his eyes and ears at the end of long wires; his own nerves, so to speak, spread over a city in the form of telephones and telegraphs. A great modern city will become a great machine with its handle in the human hand. Thus only can a man become a giant."

John Mallow looked at the man rather darkly for a moment, and then said:

"If you are so very fond of a big modern city," he said, "why do you hide yourself in such a quiet little hole in the country?"

For a flash the stranger's face seemed to wince and alter in the white sunlight; but the next instant he was still smiling, though he spoke a little more apologetically.

"There is certainly more space," he answered. "I confess I like a lot of space. But even there the science of the city will ultimately provide its own remedy. The answer is in one word – aviation."

Before the other could reply the speaker went on, his prominent eye kindling and his whole figure filling out with animation. He made a movement with his hand like a man throwing a stone into the air.

"It's upwards the new extension will be," he cried. "That road is wide enough, and that window is always open. The new roads will stand up like towers. The new harbours will stand far out in that sea above our heads – a sea you can never find the end of. It would only be a beginning to conquer the planets and colonize the fixed stars."

"I think," said Mallow, "that you will have conquered the remotest star before you really conquer this one old corner of the earth. It has a magic of its own which I think will outlast all such conjuring tricks. This was the house of Merlin; and, though they say Merlin himself fell under a spell, it was not that of Marconi."

"No," answered the stranger, still smiling. "We all know the spell under which Merlin fell."

Mallow knew enough about Russian intellectuals not to be surprised at the wide knowledge of the poetry and culture of the West; but here it seemed the almost satiric symbol of a deeper familiarity, and a mocking whisper told him what might have chained this magician in that western valley.

Laura Verney was coming across the garden towards them with some papers in her hand. She was of a red-haired, full-blooded type, handsome in a fashion which seemed to have a certain pagan exuberance till she came near enough to show the concentrated seriousness of her clear eyes; she might be called a pagan with the eyes of a puritan. She saluted her guests without any change of countenance, and handed the papers to the professor without any word of comment. Something in her automatic manner seemed to sting Mallow to a final impatience; and, picking up his hat from the window-sill, he called out in a loud and careless voice: "Laura, will you show me the way out of this garden? I've forgotten the way."

It was some time afterwards, however, that he said any sort of final farewell to her, under the shadow of the outer wall, and near the ultimate gate of the garden. In the somewhat bitter intensity of his mood, he seemed rather to be exaggerating the finality of the farewell; not only touching herself, but all the things which he had always felt to be full of her presence.

"You will pull down that old swing, I suppose?" he had said as they went through the garden, "and put up an electric steel swing that will take anybody in ten seconds to the moon."

"I can't pull down the moon, anyhow," replied the girl, with a smile, "and I don't know that I want to."

"That's rather reactionary of you," remarked Mallow. "The moon is a very extinct volcano, valuable only to old-fashioned romanticists. And I suppose you'll turn our old lawn-tennis lawn into a place where tennis can be played by machinery, by pressing buttons a hundred miles away. I'm not sure whether they've yet finished the plans for a pear tree that grows pears by electricity."

"But surely," she replied, looking a little troubled, "the world can go on without losing the things it seems to leave behind. And, after all, surely the world must go on; at least, it must go on growing. I think that's where you misunderstand. It isn't only going on; it's more like growing outwards.

"It's expansion, that's the word; growing broader, always describing wider and wider circles; but that only means more self-fulfilment, and therefore serenity and peace; it means – "

She stopped short, as if at a spoken answer, but it was only because the moon had flung a new shadow across her. It was from a figure standing on the wall. The moonshine made a halo of pale yellow round the head; and for a moment they thought it was the Russian, standing on the wall as he had stood on the roof. Then Mallow looked more closely at the face in shadow, and uttered, with some astonishment, the name of Gale.

"You must get away from here at once," said the poet sharply; "everybody who can must get away from this house. There's no time to explain."

As he spoke, he sprang from the wall and alighted beside them, and his friend, catching his face in a new light, saw that it was quite pale.

"What's the matter with you?" he demanded. "Have you seen a ghost?"

"The ghost of a fish," answered the poet; "three little grey ghosts of three little fishes. We must get away at once."

Without turning his head again, he led the way up the rising ground beyond the garden towards the clump of trees where the party had first encamped. Both Mallow and the girl pursued him with questions; but to only one of them did he give any answer. When Laura insisted on knowing whether her mother had come home yet, he answered shortly, "No; thank God! I sent Garth off to stop her on the road from the village. She's all right, anyhow."

But Laura Verney was a lady who could not be indefinitely dragged at the tail of a total stranger talking in a tone of authority; and by the time they came to the top of a hill, and the trees in whose shadow the poet had indulged in his meditations on birds, she halted and resolutely demanded his reasons.

"I won't go a step farther," she said firmly, "till you've given me some sort of proofs."

He turned with passion in his pale face.

"Oh, proofs!" he cried; "I know the sort of proofs you want. The footprints of the remarkable boots. The bloody finger-print carefully compared with the one at Scotland Yard. The conveniently mislaid matchbox, and the ashes of the unique tobacco. Do you suppose I've never read any detective stories? Well, I haven't got any proofs – of that sort. I haven't got any proofs at all, in that sense. If I told you my reasons, you'd think them the most rambling nonsense in the world. You must either do as I tell you and thank me afterwards; or you must let me talk as I like, and as long as I like, and thank your God you've come as far as this towards safety."

Mallow was looking at the poet in his quiet and intense fashion; and after a moment's pause, he said: "You'd better tell us your own reasons in your own way. I know you generally have pretty good ones, really."

Gale's eyes wandered from the staring face of the girl to that of his friend, and then to the drift of dead leaves under the tree where he had once rested.

"I was lying there looking up at the sky, or, rather, the treetops," he said slowly. "I didn't hear what the others were talking about, because I was listening to the birds and looking at them. You know what happens when you go on staring at something like that; it turns into a sort of pattern like a wallpaper; and this was a quiet pattern of green and grey and brown. It seemed as if the whole world was that pattern; as if God had never made anything except a world of birds; of treetops hung in space."

Laura made a half-protest that sounded like a laugh, but Mallow said steadily: "Go on!"

"And then I slowly became conscious that there was a spot of yellow in the pattern. I slowly realized that it was another bird, and then what sort of bird. Somebody said it must be a yellow hammer; but, little as I knew about it, I knew better than that. It was a canary."

The girl, who had already turned away, looked back at him with her first flash of interest.

"I wondered vaguely how a canary would get on in the world of birds, and how it had got there. I didn't think of any human being in particular. Only I saw in a sort of vision, somewhere against the morning sky, a window standing open, and the door of a cage standing open. Then I saw that all the brown birds were trying to kill the yellow one, and that started my thoughts off as it might anybody's. Is it always kind to set a bird at liberty? What exactly is liberty? First and foremost, surely, it is the power of a thing to be itself. In some ways the yellow bird was free in the cage. It was free to be alone. It was free to sing. In the forest its feathers would be torn to pieces and its voice choked for ever. Then I began to think that being oneself, which is liberty, is itself limitation. We are limited by our brains and bodies; and if we break out, we cease to be ourselves, and, perhaps, to be anything. That was when I asked you whether an isosceles triangle felt itself in prison, and if there were such a thing as a round prison. We shall hear more of the round prison before this story is over.

"Then I saw the man on the roof, with his hands spread like wings to the sky. I knew nothing of him; but I knew on the instant that he was the man who had given a bird its freedom at any risk. As we went down the hill I heard a little more about him; how he had escaped by blowing up his prison; and I felt that one fact had filled all his life with a philosophy of emancipation and escape. Always at the back of his mind, I was certain, was that one bursting moment when he saw white daylight shining through the shattered wall. I knew why he let birds out of cages and why he had written a book on the psychology of liberty. Then I stopped outside a window to stare at those gorgeous goldfish, merely because I had a fancy for such things; they coloured my thoughts, so to speak, with a sort of orange or scarlet, for long afterwards. And long afterwards I was again passing that window; and I found their colours were faded and their positions changed. At that time it was already dark, with a rising moon; and what forms I could see scattered in the shadow seemed almost grey, and even outlined in lines of grey light, which might have been moonlight, but I think was the corpse-light of phosphorescence. They lay scattered at random on the round table; and I saw by the faint glimmer that the glass bowl was broken. So I found my romance when I returned to it; for those fantastic fishes had been to me like the hieroglyphics of a message, which the fiery finger of God had thus written in red-hot gold. But when I looked again, the finger had written another lesson in letters of an awful and ashen silver. And what the new message said was: 'The man is mad.'

"Perhaps you think I am as mad as he; and I have told you that I am at once like him and unlike him. I am like him because I also can go on the wild journeys of such wild minds, and have a sympathy with his love of liberty. I am unlike him because, thank God, I can generally find my way home again. The lunatic is he who loses his way and cannot return. Now, almost before my eyes, this man had made the great stride from liberty to lunacy. The man who opened the birdcage loved freedom; possibly too much; certainly very much. But the man who broke the bowl merely because he thought it a prison for the fish, when it was their only possible house of life – that man was already outside the world of reason, raging with a desire to be outside everything. In a most literal and living sense, he was out of his wits. And there was another thing revealed to me by the grey ghosts of the fishes. The rise of the insanity had been very rapid and steep. To send the bird into danger was only a disputable kindness, to fling the fish to death was a dance of raving destruction. What would he do next?

"I have spoken of a round prison. After all, to any mind that can move parallel to a mood like this, there really is a round prison. The sky itself, studded with stars, the serene arch of what we call infinity – "

As he spoke he staggered, clutched at the air, and fell all his great length on the grass. At the same moment Mallow was hurled against a tree, and the girl collapsed against him, clinging to him in a way which even in that blinding whirl, was an answer to many of his questionings. It was only when they had picked themselves up and pulled themselves together that they were fully conscious that the valley was still resounding with echoes of one hideous and rending uproar; or that the darkness had just shut down upon a blaze that blinded them like red lightning. For the instant that it lasted it was a standing glory, like a great sunrise. There rose to the surface of Mallow's memory only one word for it; the word radiant.

Mallow found himself reflecting in a dull fashion that it was lighter than it might have been at that hour, because of a friendly flame that was licking itself in a lively fashion a few yards away. Then he saw that it was the smouldering ruin of the blue wooden gatepost at which he had gazed that morning, flung all the way through the air like a flaming thunderbolt. They had come just far enough from the house to be out of danger. Then he looked again at the blue-painted wood curling with golden flames, and for the first time began to tremble.

The next moment he caught sight of the faces of his other friends, Walton and Hutton, pale in the flame as they hurried up the road from the remoter inn to which they had retired for the evening.

"What was it?" Walton was calling out.

"An explosion," said Hutton rather hazily.

"An expansion," replied Mallow, and mastered himself with the effort of a grim smile.

By this time, more people were running out from remote cottages, and Gabriel Gale turned his face to something like a small crowd.

"It was only the prison gun," he said, "the signal that a prisoner has escaped."

III

THE SHADOW OF THE SHARK

It is notable that the late Mr Sherlock Holmes, in the course of those inspiring investigations for which we can never be sufficiently grateful to their ingenious author, seems only twice to have ruled out an explanation as intrinsically impossible. And it is curious to notice that in both cases the distinguished author himself has since come to regard that impossible thing as possible, and even as positively true. In the first case the great detective declared that he never knew a crime committed by a flying creature. Since the development of aviation, and especially the development of German aviation, Sir Arthur Conan Doyle, patriot and war historian, has seen a good many crimes committed by flying creatures. And in the other case the detective implied that no deed need be attributed to spirits or supernatural beings; in short, to any of the agencies to which Sir Arthur is now the most positive and even passionate witness. Presumably, in his present mood and philosophy, the Hound of the Baskervilles might well have been a really ghostly hound; at least, if the optimism which seems to go with spiritualism would permit him to believe in such a thing as a hell-hound. It may be worthwhile to note this coincidence, however, in telling a tale in which both these explanations necessarily played a part. The scientists were anxious to attribute it to aviation, and the spiritualists to attribute it to spirits; though it might be questioned whether either the spirit or the flying-man should be congratulated on his utility as an assassin.

A mystery which may yet linger as a memory, but which was in its time a sensation, revolved round the death of a certain Sir Owen Cram, a wealthy eccentric, chiefly known as a patron of learning and the arts. And the peculiarity of the case was that he was found stabbed in the middle of a great stretch of yielding sand by the seashore, on which there was absolutely no trace of any footprints but his own. It was admitted that the wound could not have been self-inflicted; and it grew more and more difficult even to suggest how it could have been inflicted at all. Many theories were suggested, ranging, as we have said, from that of the enthusiasts for aviation to that of the enthusiasts for psychical research; it being evidently regarded as a feather in the cap either of science or spiritualism to have effected so neat an operation. The true story of this strange business has never been told; it certainly contained elements which, if not supernatural, were at least supernormal. But to make it clear, we must go back to the scene with which it began; the scene on the lawn of Sir Owen's seaside residence, where the old gentleman acted as a sort of affable umpire in the disputes of the young students who were his favourite company; the scene which led up to the singular silence and isolation, and ultimately to the rather eccentric exit of Mr Amos Boon.

Mr Amos Boon had been a missionary, and still dressed like one; at any rate, he dressed like nothing else. His sturdy, full-bearded figure carried a broad-brimmed hat combined with a frock-coat; which gave him an air at once outlandish and dowdy. Though he was no longer a missionary, he was still a traveller. His face was brown and his long beard was black; there was a furrow of thought in his brow and a rather strained look in his eyes, one of which sometimes looked a little larger than the other, giving a sinister touch to what was in some ways so commonplace. He had ceased to be a missionary through what

47

he himself would have called the broadening of his mind. Some said there had been a broadening of his morals as well as of his mind; and that the South Sea Islands, where he had lived, had seen not a little of such ethical emancipation. But this was possibly a malicious misrepresentation of his very human curiosity and sympathy in the matter of the customs of the savages; which to the ordinary prejudice was indistinguishable from a white man going *fantee*. Anyhow, travelling about alone with nothing but a big Bible, he had learned to study it minutely, first for oracles and commandments, and afterwards for errors and contradictions; for the Bible-smasher is only the Bible-worshipper turned upside down. He pursued the not very arduous task of proving that David and Saul did not on all occasions merit the Divine favour; and always concluded by roundly declaring that he preferred the Philistines. Boon and his Philistines were already a byword of some levity among the young men who, at that moment, were arguing and joking around him.

At that moment Sir Owen Cram was playfully presiding over a dispute between two or three of his young friends about science and poetry. Sir Owen was a little restless man, with a large head, a bristly grey moustache, and a grey fan of hair like the crest of a cockatoo. There was something sprawling and splayfooted about his continuous movement which was compared by thoughtless youth to that of a crab; and it corresponded to a certain universal eagerness which was really ready to turn in all directions. He was a typical amateur, taking up hobby after hobby with equal inconsistency and intensity. He had impetuously left all his money to a museum of natural history, only to become immediately swallowed up in the single pursuit of landscape painting; and the groups around him largely represented the stages of his varied career. At the moment a young painter, who was also by way of being a poet, was defending some highly poetical notions against the smiling resistance of a rising doctor, whose hobby was biology. The data of agreement would have been difficult to find, and few save Sir Owen could have claimed any common basis of sympathy; but the important matter just then was the curious effect of the young men's controversy upon Mr Boon.

"The subject of flowers is hackneyed, but the flowers are not," the poet was insisting. "Tennyson was right about the flower in the crannied wall; but most people don't look at flowers in a wall, but only in a wallpaper. If you generalize them, they are dull, but if you simply see them they are always startling. If there's a special providence in a falling star, there's more in a rising star; and a live star at that."

"Well, I can't see it," said the man of science, good-humouredly; he was a red-haired, keen-faced youth in pince-nez, by the name of Wilkes. "I'm afraid we fellows grow out of the way of seeing it like that. You see, a flower is only a growth like any other, with organs and all that; and its inside isn't any prettier or uglier than an animal's. An insect is much the same pattern of rings and radiations. I'm interested in it as I am in an octopus or any sea-beast you would think a monster."

"But why should you put it that way round?" retorted the poet. "Why isn't it quite as logical the other way round? Why not say the octopus is as wonderful as the flower, instead of the flower as ordinary as the octopus? Why not say that crackens and cuttles and all the sea-monsters are themselves flowers; fearful and wonderful flowers in that terrible twilight garden of God. I do not doubt that God can be as fond of a shark as I am of a buttercup."

"As to God, my dear Gale," began the other quietly, and then he seemed to change his form of words. "Well, I am only a man – nay, only a scientific man, which you may think lower than a sea-beast. And the only interest I have in a shark is to cut him up; always on the preliminary supposition that I have prevented him from cutting me up."

"Have you ever met a shark?" asked Amos Boon, intervening suddenly.

"Not in society," replied the poet with a certain polite discomposure, looking round with something like a flush under his fair hair; he was a long, loose-limbed man named Gabriel Gale, whose pictures were more widely known than his poems.

"You've seen them in the tanks, I suppose," said Boon; "but I've seen them in the sea. I've seen them where they are lords of the sea, and worshipped by the people as great gods. I'd as soon worship those gods as any other."

Gale the poet was silent, for his mind always moved in a sort of sympathy with merely imaginative pictures; and he instantly saw, as in a vision, boiling purple seas and plunging monsters. But another young man standing near him, who had hitherto been rather primly silent, cut in quietly; a theological student, named Simon, the deposit of some epoch of faith in Sir Owen's stratified past. He was a slim man with sleek, dark hair and darting, mobile eyes, in spite of his compressed lips. Whether in caution or contempt, he had left the attack on medical materialism to the poet, who was always ready to plunge into an endless argument with anybody. Now he intervened merely to say:

"Do they only worship a shark? It seems rather a limited sort of religion."

"Religion!" repeated Amos Boon, rudely; "what do you people know about religion? You pass the plate round, and when Sir Owen puts a penny in it, you put up a shed where a curate can talk to a congregation of maiden aunts. These people have got something like a religion. They sacrifice things to it – their beasts, their babies, their lives. I reckon you'd turn green with fear if you'd ever so much as caught a glimpse of Religion. Oh, it's not just a fish in the sea; rather it's the sea round a fish. The sea is the blue cloud he moves in, or the green veil or curtain hung about him, the skirts of which trail with thunder."

All faces were turned towards him, for there was something about him beyond his speech. Twilight was spreading over the garden, which lay near the edge of a chalk cliff above the shore, but the last light of sunset still lay on a part of the lawn, painting it yellow rather than green, and glowing almost like gold against the last line of the sea, which was a sombre indigo and violet, changing nearer land to a lurid, pale green. A long cloud of a jagged shape happened to be trailing across the sun; and the broad-hatted, hairy man from the South Seas suddenly pointed at it.

"I know where the shape of that cloud would be called the shadow of the shark," he cried, "and a thousand men would fall on their faces ready to fast or fight, or die. Don't you see the great black dorsal fin, like the peak of a moving mountain? And then you lads discuss him as if he were a stroke at golf; and one of you says he would cut him up like birthday cake; and the other says your Jewish Jehovah would condescend to pat him like a pet rabbit."

"Come, come," said Sir Owen, with a rather nervous waggishness, "we mustn't have any of your broad-minded blasphemies."

Boon turned on him a baneful eye; literally an eye, for one of his eyes grew larger till it glowed like the eye of the Cyclops. His figure was black against the fiery turf, and they could almost hear his beard bristling.

"Blasphemy!" he cried in a new voice, with a crack in it. "Take care it is not you who blaspheme."

And then, before anyone could move, the black figure against the patch of gold had swung round and was walking away from the house, so impetuously that they had a momentary fear that he would walk over the cliff. However, he found the little wooden gate that led to a flight of wooden steps; and they heard him stumbling down the path to the fishing village below.

Sir Owen seemed suddenly to shake off a paralysis like a fit of slumber. "My old friend is a little eccentric," he said. "Don't go, gentlemen; don't let him break up the party. It is early yet."

But growing darkness and a certain social discomfort had already begun to dissolve the group on the lawn; and the host was soon left with a few of the most intimate of his guests. Simon and Gale, and his late antagonist, Dr Wilkes, were staying to dinner; the darkness drove them indoors, and eventually found them sitting round a flask of green Chartreuse on the table; for Sir Owen had his expensive conventions as well as his expensive eccentricities. The talkative poet, however, had fallen silent, and was staring at the green liquid in his glass as if it were the green depth of the sea. His host attacked with animation the other ordinary topics of the day.

"I bet I'm the most industrious of the lot of you," he said. "I've been at my easel on the beach all day, trying to paint this blessed cliff, and make it look like chalk and not cheese."

"I saw you, but I didn't like to disturb you," said Wilkes. "I generally try to put in an hour or so looking for specimens at high tide: I suppose most people think I'm shrimping or only paddling and doing it for my health. But I've got a pretty good nucleus of that museum we were talking about, or at least the aquarium part of it. I put in most of the rest of the time arranging the exhibits; so I deny the implication of idleness. Gale was on the seashore, too. He was doing nothing as usual; and now he's saying nothing, which is much more uncommon."

"I have been writing letters," said Simon, in his precise way, "but letters are not always trivial. Sometimes they are rather tremendous."

Sir Owen glanced at him for a moment, and a silence followed, which was broken by a thud and a rattle of glasses as Gale brought his fist down on the table like a man who had thought of something suddenly.

"Dagon!" he cried, in a sort of ecstasy.

Most of the company seemed but little enlightened; perhaps they thought that saying "Dagon" was his poetical and professional fashion of saying "Damn." But the dark eyes of Simon brightened, and he nodded quickly.

"Why, of course you're right," he said. "That must be why Mr Boon is so fond of the Philistines."

In answer to a general stare of inquiry, he said smoothly: "The Philistines were a people from Crete, probably of Hellenic origin, who settled on the coast of Palestine, carrying with them a worship which may very well have been that of Poseidon, but which their enemies, the Israelites, described as that of Dagon. The relevant matter here is that the carved or painted symbol of the god seems always to have been a fish."

The mention of the new matter seemed to reawaken the tendency of the talk to turn into a wrangle between the poet and the professional scientist.

"From my point of view," said the latter. "I must confess myself somewhat disappointed with your friend Mr Boon. He represented himself as a rationalist like myself, and seemed to have made some scientific studies of folklore in the South Seas. But he seemed a little unbalanced; and surely he made a curious fuss about some sort of a fetish, considering it was only a fish."

"No, no, no!" cried Gale, almost with passion. "Better make a fetish of the fish. Better sacrifice yourself and everybody else on the horrible huge altar of the fish. Better do anything than utter the star-blasting blasphemy of saying it is *only* a fish. It's as bad as saying the other thing is only a flower."

"All the same, it *is* only a flower," answered Wilkes, "and the advantage of looking at these things in a cool and rational way from the outside is that you can – "

He stopped a moment and remained quite still, as if he were watching something. Some even fancied that his pale, aquiline face looked paler as well as sharper.

"What was that at the window?" he asked. "Is anybody outside this house?"

"What's the matter? What did you see?" asked his host, in abrupt agitation.

"Only a face," replied the doctor, "but it was not – it was not like a man's face. Let's get outside and look into this."

Gabriel Gale was only a moment behind the doctor, who had impetuously dashed out of the room. Despite his lounging demeanour, the poet had already leapt to his feet with his hand on the back of the chair, when he stiffened where he stood; for he had seen it. The faces of the others showed that they had seen it too.

Pressed against the dark windowpane, but only wanly luminous as it protruded out of the darkness, was a large face looking at first rather like a green goblin mask in a pantomime. Yet it was in no sense human; its eyes were set in large circles, rather in the fashion of an owl. But the glimmering covering that faintly showed on it was not of feathers, but of scales.

The next moment it had vanished. The mind of the poet, which made images as rapidly as a cinema, even in a crisis of action, had already imagined a string of fancies about the sort of creature he saw it to be. He had thought involuntarily of some great flying fish winging its way across the foam, and the flat sand and the spire and roofs of the fishing village. He had half-imagined the moist sea air thickening in some strange way to a greener and more liquid atmosphere in which the marine monsters could swim about in the streets. He had entertained the fancy that the house itself stood in the depths of the sea, and that the great goblin-headed fishes were nosing round it, as round the cabin windows of a wreck.

At that moment a loud voice was heard outside crying in distinct accents:

"The fish has legs."

For that instant, it seemed to give the last touch to the monstrosity. But the meaning of it came back to them, a returning reality, with the laughing face of Dr Wilkes as he reappeared in the doorway, panting.

"Our fish had two legs, and used them," he said. "He ran like a hare when he saw me coming; but I could see plainly enough it was a man, playing you a trick of some sort. So much for that psychic phenomenon."

He paused and looked at Sir Owen Cram with a smile that was keen and almost suspicious.

"One thing is very clear to me," he said. "You have an enemy."

The mystery of the human fish, however, did not long remain even a primary topic of conversation in a social group that had so many topics of conversation. They continued to pursue their hobbies and pelt each other with their opinions; even the smooth and silent Simon being gradually drawn into the discussions, in which he showed a dry and somewhat cynical dexterity. Sir Owen continued to paint with all the passion of an amateur. Gale continued to neglect to paint, with all the nonchalance of a painter. Mr Boon was presumably still as busy with his wicked Bible and his good Philistines as Dr Wilkes with his museum and his microscopic marine animals, when the little seaside town was shaken as by an earthquake with the incomprehensible calamity which spread its name over all the newspapers of the country.

Gabriel Gale was scaling the splendid swell of turf that terminated in the great chalk cliff above the shore, in a mood consonant to the sunrise that was storming the skies above him. Clouds haloed with sunshine were already sailing over his head as if sent flying from a flaming wheel; and when he came to the brow of the cliff he saw one of those rare revelations when the sun does not seem to be merely the most luminous object in a luminous landscape, but itself the solitary focus and streaming fountain of all light. The tide was at the ebb, and the sea was only a strip of delicate turquoise over which rose the tremendous irradiation. Next to the strip of turquoise was a strip of orange sand, still wet, and nearer the sand was a desert of a more dead yellow or brown, growing paler in the increasing light. And as he looked down from the precipice upon that plain of pale gold, he saw two black objects lying in the middle of it. One was a small easel, still standing, with a camp-stool fallen beside it; the other was the flat and sprawling figure of a man.

The figure did not move, but as he stared he became conscious that another human figure was moving, was walking over the flat sands towards it from under the shadow of the cliff. Looking at it steadily, he saw that it was the man called Simon; and in an instant he seemed to realize that the motionless figure was that of Sir Owen Cram. He hastened to the stairway down the cliff and so to the sands; and soon stood face to face with Simon; for they both looked at each other for a moment before they both looked down at the body. The conviction was already cold in his heart that it was a dead body. Nevertheless, he said sharply: "We must have a doctor; where is Dr Wilkes?"

"It is no good, I fear," said Simon, looking away at the sea.

"Wilkes may only confirm our fears that he is dead," said Gale, "but he may have something to say about how he died."

"True," said the other, "I will go for him myself." And he walked back rapidly towards the cliff in the track of his own footprints.

Indeed, it was at the footprints that Gale was gazing in a bemused fashion at that moment. The tracks of his own coming were clear enough, and the tracks of Simon's coming and going; and the third rather more rambling track of the unmistakable boots of the unfortunate Sir Owen, leading up to the spot where his easel was planted. And that was all. The sand was soft, so that the lightest foot would disturb it; it was well above the tides; and there was not the faintest trace of any other human being having been near the body. Yet the body had a deep wound under the angle of the jaw; and there was no sign of any weapon of suicide.

Gabriel Gale was a believer in common sense, in theory if not always in practice. He told himself repeatedly that these things were the practical clues in such a case; the wound, the weapon or absence of weapon, the footprints or absence of footprints. But there was also a part of his mind which was always escaping from his control and playing tricks; fixing on his memory meaningless things as if they were symbols, and then haunting him with them as mysteries. He made no point of it; it was rather sub-conscious than self-conscious; but the parts of any living picture that he saw were seldom those that others saw, or that it seemed sensible to see. And there were one or two details in the tragedy before him that haunted him then and long afterwards. Cram had fallen backwards in a rather twisted fashion, with his feet towards the shore; and a few inches from the left foot lay a starfish. He could not say whether it was merely the bright orange colour of the creature that irrationally rivetted his eye, or merely some obscure fancy of repetition, in that the human figure was itself spread and sprawling flat like a starfish, with four limbs instead of five. Nor did he attempt to analyse this aesthetic antic of his psychology; it was a suppressed part of his mind which still repeated that the mystery of the untrodden sands would turn out to be something quite simple; but that the starfish possessed the secret.

He looked up to see Simon returning with the doctor, indeed with two doctors; for there was more than one medical representative in the mob of Sir Owen's varied interests. The other was a Dr Garth, a little man with an angular and humorous face; he was an old friend of Gale's, but the poet's greeting was rather *distrait*. Garth and his colleagues, however, got to work on a preliminary examination, which made further talk needless. It could not be a full examination till the arrival of the police, but it was sufficient to extinguish any hope of life, if any such had lingered. Garth, who was bent over the body in a crouching posture, spoke to his fellow physician without raising his head.

"There seems to be something rather odd about this wound. It goes almost straight upwards, as if it was struck from below. But Sir Owen was a very small man; and it seems queer that he should be stabbed by somebody smaller still."

Gale's sub-consciousness exploded with a strange note of harsh mockery.

"What," he cried, "you don't think the starfish jumped up and killed him?"

"No, of course not," said Garth, with his gruff good humour. "What on earth is the matter with you?"

"Lunacy, I think," said the poet, and began to walk slowly towards the shore.

As time went on he almost felt disposed to fancy that he had correctly diagnosed his own complaint. The image began to figure even in his dreams, but not merely as a natural nightmare about the body on the seashore. The significant sea creature seemed more vivid even than the body. As he had originally seen the corpse from above, spread flat out beneath him, he saw it in his visions as something standing, as if propped against a wall or even merely drawn or graven on a wall. Sometimes the sandy ground had become a ground of old gold in some decoration of the Dark Ages, with the figure in the stiff agonies of a martyr, but the red star always showed like a lamp by his feet. Sometimes it was a hieroglyphic of a more Eastern sort, as of some stone god rigidly dancing; but the five-pointed star was always in the same place below. Sometimes it seemed a rude, red sandstone sort of drawing; yet more archaic; but the star was always the reddest spot in it. Now and again, while the human figure was as dry and dark as a mummy, the star would seem to be literally alive, waving its flaming fingers as if it were trying to tell him something. Now and then even the whole figure was upside down, as if to restore the star to its proper place in the skies.

"I told Wilkes that a flower was a living star," he said to himself. "A starfish is more literally a living star. But this is like going crazy. And if there is one thing I strongly object to, it is going crazy. What use should I be to all my brother lunatics, if I once really lost my balance on the tightrope over the abyss?"

He sat staring into vacancy for some time, trying to fit in this small and stubborn fancy with a much steadier stream of much deeper thoughts that were already driving in a certain direction. At last, the light of a possibility began to dawn in his eyes; and it was evidently something very simple when it was realized; something which he felt he ought to have thought of before; for he laughed shortly and scornfully at himself as he rose to his feet.

"If Boon goes about everywhere introducing his shark and I go into society always attended by my starfish," he murmured to himself, "we shall turn the world into an aquarium bigger and better than Dr Wilkes is fixing up. I'm going down to make some inquiries in the village."

Returning thence across the sands at evening, after several conversations with skippers and fishermen, he wore a more satisfied expression.

"I always did believe," he reflected, "that the footprint business would be the simplest thing in the affair. But there are some things in it that are by no means simple."

Then he looked up, and saw far off on the sands, lonely and dark against the level evening light, the strange hat and stumpy figure of Amos Boon.

He seemed to consider for a moment the advisability of a meeting; then he turned away and moved towards the stairway up the cliff. Mr Boon was apparently occupied in idly drawing lines on the sand with his shabby umbrella; like one drawing plans for a child's sandcastle, but apparently without any such intelligent object or excuse. Gale had often seen the man mooning about with equally meaningless and automatic gestures; but as the poet mounted the rocky steps, climbing higher and higher, he had a return of the irrational feeling of a visionary vertigo. He told himself again, as if in warning, that it was his whole duty in life to walk on a tightrope above a void in which many imaginative men were swallowed up. Then he looked down again at the drop of the dizzy cliffs to the flats that seemed to be swimming below him like a sea. And he saw the long, loose lines drawn in the sand unified into a shape, as flat as a picture on a wall. He had often seen a child, in the same fashion, draw on the sand a pig as large as a house. But in this case he could not shake off his former feeling of something archaic, like a palaeolithic drawing, about the scratching of the brown sand. And Mr Boon had not drawn a pig, but a shark; conspicuous with its jagged teeth and fin like a horn exalted.

But he was not the only person overlooking this singular decorative scheme. When he came to the short railings along the brow of the cliff in which the stairway terminated, he found three figures leaning on it and looking down; and instantly realized how the case was closing in. For even in their outlines against the sky he had recognized the two doctors and an inspector of police.

"Hullo, Gale," observed Wilkes, "may I present you to Inspector Davies; a very active and successful officer."

Garth nodded. "I understand the inspector will soon make an arrest," he said.

"The inspector must be getting back to his work and not talking about it," said that official good-humouredly. "I'm going down to the village. Anybody coming my way?"

Dr Wilkes assented and followed him, but Dr Garth stopped a moment, being detained by the poet, who caught hold of his sleeve with unusual earnestness.

"Garth," he said, "I want to apologise. I'm afraid I was wool-gathering when we met the other day, and didn't hail you as I ought to hail an old friend. You and I have been in one or two queer affairs together, and I want to talk to you about this one. Shall we sit down on that seat over there?"

They seated themselves on an iron seat set up on the picturesque headland; and Gale added, "I wish you could tell me roughly how you got as far as you seem to have got."

Garth gazed silently out to sea, and said at last:

"Do you know that man Simon?"

"Yes," replied the poet, "that's the way it works is it?"

"Well, the investigation soon began to show that Simon knew rather more than he said. He was on the spot before you; and for some time he wouldn't admit what it was he saw before you turned up. We guessed it was because he was afraid to tell the truth; and in one sense he was."

"Simon doesn't talk enough," said Gale thoughtfully. "He doesn't talk about himself enough; so he thinks about himself too much. A man like that always gets secretive; not necessarily in the sense of being criminal, or even of being malicious, but merely of being morbid. He is the sort that is ill-treated at school and never says so. As long as a thing terrified him, he couldn't talk about it."

"I don't know how you guessed it," said Garth, "but that is something like the line of discoveries. At first they thought that Simon's silence was guilt, but it was only a fear of something more than guilt; of some diabolic destiny and entanglement. The truth is, that when he went up before you to the cliff head at daybreak, he saw something that hag-rode his morbid spirit ever since. He saw the figure of this man Boon poised on the brink of the precipice, black against the dawn, and waving his arms in some unearthly fashion as if he were going to fly. Simon thought the man was talking to himself, and perhaps even singing. Then the strange creature passed on towards the village and was lost in the twilight; but when Simon came to the edge of the cliff he saw Sir Owen lying dead far out on the sands below, beside his easel."

"And ever since, I suppose," observed Gale, "Simon has seen sharks everywhere."

"You are right again," said the doctor. "He has admitted since that a shadow on the blind or a cloud on the moon would have the unmistakable shape of the fish with the fin erect. But, in fact, it is a very mistakable shape; anything with a triangular top to it would suggest it to a man in his state of nerves. But the truth is that so long as he thought Boon had dealt death from a distance by some sort of curse or spell, we could get nothing out of him. Our only chance was to show him that Boon might have done it even by natural means. And we did show it, after all."

"What is your theory, then?" asked the other.

"It is too general to be called a theory yet," replied the doctor; "but, honestly, I do not think it at all impossible that Boon might have killed a man on the sands from the top of a cliff, without falling back on any supernatural stuff. You've got to consider it like this: Boon has been very deep in the secrets of savages, especially in that litter of islands that lie away towards Australia. Now, we know that such savages, for all they are called ignorant, have developed many dexterities and many unique tools. They have blow-pipes that kill at a considerable distance; they harpoon and lasso things, and draw them in on a line. Above all, the Australian savages have discovered the boomerang that actually returns to the hand. Is it quite so inconceivable that Boon might know some way of sending a penetrating projectile from a distance, and even possibly of recovering it in some way? Dr Wilkes and I, on examining the wound, found it a very curious one: it was made by some tapering, pointed tool, with a slight curve; and it not only curved upwards, but even slightly outwards, as if the curve were returning on itself. Does not that suggest to you some outlandish weapon of a strange shape, and possibly with strange properties? And always remember that such an explanation would explain something else as well, which is generally regarded as the riddle. It would explain why the murderer left no footprints round the body."

Gale gazed out to sea in silence, as if considering; then he said simply: "An extremely shrewd argument. But I know why he left no footprints. It is a much simpler explanation than that."

Garth stared at him for a few moments; and then observed gravely: "May I then ask, in return, what is your theory?"

"My theory will seem a maze of theories, and nothing else," said Gale. "It is, as many would say, of such stuff as dreams are made of. Most modern people have a curious contradiction; they abound in theories, yet they never see the part that theories play in practical life. They are always talking about temperament and circumstances and accident; but most men are what their theories make them; most men go in for murder or marriage, or mere lounging because of some theory of life, asserted or assumed. So I can never manage to begin my explanations in that brisk, pointed, practical way that you doctors and detectives do. I see a man's mind first, sometimes almost without any particular man attached to it. I could only begin this business by describing a mental state – which can't be described. Our murderer or maniac, or whatever you call him, is certainly affected by some of the elements attributed to him. His view has reached an insane degree of simplicity, and in that sense of savagery. But I doubt whether he would necessarily transfer the savagery from the end to the means. In one sense, indeed, his view might be compared to the barbaric. He saw every creature and even every object naked. He did not understand that what clothes a thing is sometimes the most real part of it. Have you ever noticed how true is that old phrase, 'clothed and in his right mind'? Man is not in his right mind when he is not clothed with the symbols of his social dignity. Humanity is not even human when it is naked. But in a lower sense it is so of lesser things, even of lifeless things. A lot of nonsense is talked about auras; but this is the truth behind it.

Everything has a halo. Everything has a sort of atmosphere of what it signifies, which makes it sacred. Even the little creatures he studied had each of them its halo; but he would not see it."

"But what little creatures did Boon study?" asked Garth in some wonder. "Do you mean the cannibals?"

"I was not thinking about Boon," replied Gabriel Gale.

"What do you mean?" cried the other, in sudden excitement. "Why, Boon is almost in the hands of the police."

"Boon is a good man," said Gale, calmly; "he is very stupid; that is why he is an atheist. There are intelligent atheists, as we shall see presently; but that stunted, stupid sort is much commoner, and much nicer. But he is a good man; his motive is good; he originally talked all that tosh of the superiority of the savage because he thought he was the underdog. He may be a trifle cracked, by now, about sharks and other things; but that's only because his travels have been too much for his intellect. They say travel broadens the mind; but you must have the mind. He had a mind for a suburban chapel, and there passed before it all the panorama of gilded nature-worship and purple sacrifice. He doesn't know if he's on his head or his heels, any more than a good many others. But I shouldn't wonder if heaven is largely populated with atheists of that sort, scratching their heads and wondering where they are.

"But Boon is a parenthesis; that is all he is. The man I am talking about is very much the point, and a sharp one at that. He dealt in something very different from muddled mysticism about human sacrifice. Human sacrifice is quite a human weakness. He dealt in assassination; direct, secret, straight from a head as inhuman as hell. And I knew it when I first talked to him over the teacups and he said he saw nothing pretty in a flower."

"My dear fellow!" remonstrated Dr Garth.

"I don't mean that a man merely dissecting a daisy must be on the road to the gallows," conceded the poet, magnanimously, "but I do say that to mean it as he meant it is to be on a straight road of logic that leads there if he chooses to follow it. God is inside everything. But this man wanted to be outside everything; to see everything hung in a vacuum, simply its own dead self. It's not only not the same, it's almost the opposite of scepticism in the sense of Boon or the Book of Job. That's a man overwhelmed by the mysteries; but this man denies that there are any mysteries. It's not, in the ordinary sense, a matter of theology, but psychology. Most good pagans and pantheists might talk of the miracles of nature; but this man denies that there are any miracles, even in the sense of marvels. Don't you see that dreadful dry light shed on things must at last wither up the moral mysteries as illusions, respect for age, respect for property, and that the sanctity of life will be a superstition? The men in the street are only organisms, with their organs more or less displayed. For such a one there is no longer any terror in the touch of human flesh, nor does he see God watching him out of the eyes of a man."

"He may not believe in miracles, but he seems to work them," remarked the doctor. "What else was he doing, when he struck a man down on the sand without leaving a mark to show where he stood?"

"He was paddling," answered Gale.

"As high up on the shore as that?" inquired the other.

Gale nodded. "That was what puzzled me; till something I saw on the sand started a train of thought that led to my asking the seafaring people about the tides. It's very simple; the night before we found the body was a flood-tide, and the sea came up higher than usual; not quite to where Cram was sitting, but pretty near. So that was the way that the real human fish came out of the sea. That was the way the divine shark really devoured the sacrifice. The man came paddling in the foam, like a child on a holiday."

"Who came?" asked Garth; but he shuddered.

"Who did go dredging for sea-beasts with a sort of shrimping-net along the shore every evening? Who did inherit the money of the old man for his ambitious museum and his scientific career? Who did tell me in the garden that a cowslip was only a growth like a cancer?"

"I am compelled to understand you," said the doctor gloomily. "You mean that very able young man named Wilkes?"

"To understand Wilkes you must understand a good deal," continued his friend. "You must reconstruct the crime, as they say. Look out over that long line of darkening sea and sand, where the last light runs red as blood; that is where he came dredging every day, in the same bloodshot dusk, looking for big beasts and small; and in a true sense everything was fish that came to his net. He was constructing his museum as a sort of cosmos; with everything traced from the fossil to the flying fish. He had spent enormous sums on it, and had got quite disinterestedly into debt; for instance he had had magnificent models made, in wax or papier mâché, of small fish magnified, or extinct fish restored; things that South Kensington cannot afford, and certainly Wilkes could not afford. But he had persuaded Cram to leave his money to the museum, as you know; and for him Cram was simply a silly old fool, who painted pictures he couldn't paint, and talked of sciences he didn't understand; and whose only natural function was to die and save the museum. Well, when every morning Wilkes had done polishing the glass cases of his masks and models, he came round by the cliff and took a turn at the fossils in the chalk with his geological hammer; then he put it back in that great canvas bag of his, and unslung his long shrimping net and began to wade. This is where I want you to look at that dark red sand and see the picture; one never understands anything till one sees the picture. He went for miles along the shallows of that desolate shore, long inured to seeing one queer creature or another stranded on the sand; here a sea hedgehog, and there a starfish, and then a crab, and then another creature. I have told you he had reached a stage when he would have looked at an angel with the eye of an ornithologist. What would he think of a man, and a man looking like that? Don't you see that poor Cram must have looked like a crab or a sea-urchin; his dwarfed, hunched figure seen from behind, with his fan of bristling whiskers, his straggling bow legs and restless twisting feet all tangled up with the three legs of his stool; making him look as if he had five limbs like a starfish? Don't you see he looked like a Common Object of the Seashore? And Wilkes had only to collect this specimen, and all his other specimens were safe. Everything was fish that came to his net, and...

"He stretched out the long pole in his hand to its full extent, and drew the net over the old man's head as if he were catching a great grey moth. He plucked him backwards off his stool so that he lay kicking on his back on the sand; and doubtless looking more like a large insect than ever. Then the murderer bent forward, propped by one hand upon his pole, and the other armed with his geological hammer. With the pick at the back of that instrument he struck in what he well knew to be a vital spot. The curve you noticed in the wound is due to that sharp side of the hammer being shaped like a pickaxe. But the unusual position of it, and the puzzle of how such a blow could be struck upwards, was due to the queer posture of the two figures. The murderer struck at a head that was upside down. It could only occur as a rule if the victim were standing on his head, a posture in which few persons await the assassin. But with the flourish and sweep of the great net, I fancy a starfish caught in it fell out of it, just beyond the dead man's foot. At any rate, it was that starfish and the accident of its flying so high on the shore, that set my mind drifting in the general direction of tides; and the possibility of the murderer having been moving about in the water. If he made any prints the breakers washed them out; and I should never have begun to think of it but for that red five-fingered little monster."

"Then do you mean to tell me," demanded Garth, "that all this business about the shadow of the shark had nothing to do with it?"

"The shadow of the shark had everything to do with it," replied Gale. "The murderer hid in the shadow of the shark, and struck from under the shadow of the shark. I doubt if he would have struck at all, if he had not had the shadow of that fantastic fin in which to hide. And the proof is that he himself took the trouble to emphasize and exaggerate the legend of poor Boon dancing before Dagon. Do you remember that queer incident of the fish's face at the window? How did anybody merely playing a practical joke get hold of a fish's face? It was very life-like; for it was one of the masks modelled for the Wilkes museum; and Wilkes had left it in the hall in his great canvas bag. It seems simple, doesn't it, for a man to raise an alarm inside a house, walk out to see, and instantly put on a mask and look in at a window? That's all he did; and you can see his idea, from the fact that he proceeded to warn Sir Owen of an enemy. He wanted all this idolatrous and mystical murder business worked for all it was worth, that his own highly reasonable murder might not be noticed. And you see he has succeeded. You tell me that Boon is in the hands of the police."

Garth sprang to his feet. "What is to be done?" he said.

"You will know what to do," said the poet. "You are a good and just man, and a practical man, too. I am not a practical man." He rose with a certain air of apology. "You see, you want an unpractical man for finding out this sort of thing."

And once more he gazed down from the precipice into the abysses below.

IV

THE CRIME OF GABRIEL GALE

Dr Butterworth, the famous London physician, was sitting in his summerhouse in his shirt sleeves, for it was a hot day and he had been playing tennis on the sunny lawns outside. He had a solid face and figure and carried everywhere an atmosphere of bodily health and good humour which helped him not a little in his profession; but he was not serious or self-conscious about it. He was not one of those in whom health has degenerated into hygiene. He played tennis when he felt inclined and left off when he felt inclined; as on the present occasion, when he had retired to smoke a pipe in the shade. He enjoyed a game as he enjoyed a joke; which was interpreted by some as meaning that he would never be a player, and by himself as meaning that he would always be able to play. And he enjoyed a joke very much, even the most minute and trivial joke that his roving eye encountered; and at this moment it encountered a quaint detail, which was something of a quaint contrast, in the glowing garden outside. Framed in the dark doorway of the summerhouse, like a lighted scene on the stage, was the perspective of a garden path, bordered with very gay and flamboyant beds of tulips, having something of the gorgeous formality of the borders of a Persian illumination. And down the centre of the central path was advancing a figure that looked by comparison almost completely black, with black top-hat, black clothes and black umbrella; it might have been the mythical Black Tulip come to life and a walking parody of the tall, top-heavy garden flowers. The next moment all such fancies had faded from the doctor's daydream; for he had recognised a familiar face under the top hat; he knew that the contrast was not merely grotesque; and was shocked with the gravity of the visitor's eyes.

"Hullo, Garth," he said in a hearty manner, "sit down and tell us all about yourself. You look as if you were going to a funeral."

"So I am," replied Dr Garth, putting his black hat on a chair; he was a small, red haired, shrewd-faced man and he looked pale and harassed.

"I am so sorry," said Butterworth quickly, "if I spoke without thinking. I'm afraid you're really rather cut up."

"I am going to a queer sort of funeral," said Dr Garth grimly; "the sort of funeral where we take special precautions to ensure premature burial."

"What in the world do you mean?" asked his colleague, staring.

"I mean I've got to bury a man alive," said Garth with a ghastly calm. "But it's the sort of burial that requires two doctors' certificates instead of one."

Butterworth stared at the patch of sunlight and sucked in his cheeks with a soundless whistle. "Oh…I see," he said.

Then he added abruptly: "Of course it's always a sad business; but I'm afraid it's rather personal for you. A friend of yours?"

"One of my best friends, I think, barring yourself," replied Garth; "and one of the best and brightest young men of our time as well. I was afraid something of the sort might happen; but I hoped it wouldn't be so bad as this." He stopped for an instant and then said almost explosively: "It's poor old Gale; and he's done it once too often."

"Done what?" asked Dr Butterworth.

"It's rather difficult to explain, unless you know him," said Garth. "Gabriel Gale is a poet, also a painter and other wild things of that sort; but he has also a wild theory of his own about how to cure lunatics. In short, the amateur set up as a mad doctor and now the doctor is really mad. It's a horrid tragedy; but really he was asking for it."

"I don't yet understand what it's all about," said the other doctor patiently.

"I tell you he had a theory," said Garth. "He thought he could cure cracked people by what he called sympathy. But it didn't mean what you would mean by sympathy; he meant following their thoughts and going half-way with them, or all the way with them if he could. I used to joke with him, poor fellow, and say that if a lunatic thought he was made of glass, Gale would try hard to feel a little transparent. Anyhow, that was his notion, that he could really look at things to some extent from the lunatic's point of view; and talk to him in his own language. He admitted himself that it was a risky business, to walk on the edge of the precipice like that; and now, as I say, he's done it once too often. I always distrusted it myself."

"I should think so," said Dr Butterworth, all his solid sanity stiffening against the suggestion. "He might as well say that a doctor ought to limp all the way to cure a lame man, or shut his eyes in order to help the blind."

"If the blind lead the blind," assented the other gloomily. "Well, he's fallen into the ditch this time."

"Why especially this time?" asked Butterworth.

"Well, if he doesn't go to an asylum, he'll go to jail," said Garth grimly. "That's why I'm in such a hurry to have him certified; God knows I don't like doing that. But he's broken out this time in a way he never did before. He was always fanciful and eccentric, of course; but I'm bound to say he had a very sane streak in him somewhere. It's exactly because he's never done anything like this before that I'm sure the end has really come. For one thing, he's committed a perfectly crazy assault and apparently tried to murder a man with a pitchfork. But what hits me much harder, who knew him, is that he tried to murder a perfectly mild and shy and inoffensive person; in fact a rather gauche youth from Cambridge, half-developed into a curate. Now that's quite unlike Gabriel, even at his maddest. The men with whom he wrestled in spirit, if not in body, were intellectual bullies or mesmerists, the sort of men who wanted somebody to stand up to them; like that thin-lipped Dr Wilkes, or that Russian Professor. I can no more see him savaging somebody like poor young Saunders than I can see him kicking a crippled child. And yet I *did* see him do it. The only explanation is that he wasn't himself.

"There was another thing which made me sure he wasn't himself. The weather had been very trying for everybody for some time; hot and stormy and electric; but it was the first time I've ever known him upset by such storms. I've known him to do the silliest things; I've known him stand on his head in the garden; but that was only showing that he was not affected by the storm. But this time I'm sure these queer semi-tropical tempests have been too much for him; so that even the very subject of the storm upset him in some way. For this tragedy arose out of the most trivial sort of triviality. The whole terrible unnatural business began with talking about the weather.

"Lady Flamborough said to a guest at her rather damp garden-party, 'You brought bad weather with you.' Anybody might say that to anybody; but she did say it to young Herbert Saunders, who is awfully awkward and shy, one of those long, loose boys with large feet, who seem to have outgrown their clothes and their wits; the last sort of person who would want to be singled out by any remark, however trifling. So Saunders only gaped and gurgled or was dumb, but somehow the lady's remark seemed to get on Gale's nerves from the first. A little while afterwards Gale met Lady Flamborough again, at another reception where it was raining, and he suddenly pointed, like some comic conspirator, at the tall ungainly figure of Saunders in the distance and said: 'He still brings bad weather.' Then happened one of those coincidences that are quite natural but seem to drive madmen really mad. The next time all that set happened to get together was on a really beautiful afternoon at Mrs Blakeney's; with a clear blue sky without a cloud in it, so that old Blakeney went pottering round and showed all the first corners his gardens and glasshouses. But after that they all went in to tea, which was served in the great peacock-green drawing-room in the middle of the house; and so it happened that Saunders came late and there was a good deal of laughter as he sat down, much to his embarrassment; because the weather joke had been repeated and people were quite pleased to see it falsified for once. Then they all went out into the rooms nearer the entrance; and Gabriel Gale was walking towards the doorway. Between two pillars he caught sight of one of the outer windows and stood rooted to the spot, rigidly pointing with one arm. That gesture alone warned me that something was really rather wrong with him; but when I looked I could hardly help sharing his shock of surprise. For the windows that had been painted blue with summer sky were painted black with rain. On every side of the house the rain dripped and pattered as dismally as if it had been raining for a hundred years. And ten minutes before the whole garden had seemed a garden of gold like the Hesperides. Gale stood staring at this flying storm from nowhere, that had so suddenly struck the house; then he turned slowly and looked, with an expression not to be forgotten, at the man who was standing a few yards away. It was Herbert Saunders.

"You can imagine it's not much in my line to believe in witchcraft or magicians who control the elements; but there did really seem something funny about that cloudless day having so rapidly overclouded, with the coming of the one man whose name was already associated with it, if only by a jest. It was a mere coincidence, of course; but what worried me was the possible effect on my friend's already rather rickety psychology.

He and Saunders were both standing and staring out of the same wide window, looking at the deluge-darkened garden and the swaying and tormented trees; but Saunders' simple face seemed to express only amiable bewilderment; indeed, he was smiling vaguely and shyly, as he did when he received a compliment. For he was one of those whose face after a compliment always looks as if it has received a buffet. He obviously saw nothing in it but a repetition of the joke; perhaps he thought that the English climate was keeping up the joke. And, compared with his face, the face of Gabriel was like the face of a fiend. So it seemed at least, as it sprang white out of the growing dark to meet the first white burst of the lightning; then there followed only thunder and the noise of the roaring rain; but I knew that he stood there rocking with that inexplicable excitement. Through the thunder I heard his voice saying, 'It makes one feel like God.'

"Immediately under the windows a little path ran on the edge of some meadow land attached to the garden, where the Blakeneys had been getting in their hay; and a moderately large mound of hay looked almost mountainously dark against that low and lowering sky; a two-pronged pitchfork lying across it had certainly something grim about its black outline, which may have captured poor Gale's fancy; for he was always prone to be taken by odd sights as if they were signals. Anyhow at that moment the host and hostess and other guests came hurrying by; the old man lamenting over the ruin of his hay; but the lady of the house apparently much more concerned about the fate of some highly ornamental garden chairs, which had apparently been left out on the lawn just adjoining the meadow, under the large apple tree whose boughs were now tossing and twisting in the storm.

"Gabriel Gale, when in his right mind, is the most chivalrous of men, and would have regained the lady's chairs at a bound. But now he could do nothing but glare at the unfortunate Saunders; who awoke trembling to his social duties, in that agony of self-consciousness in which a man is afraid to do the right thing and afraid not to do it. At length, however, he jerked himself forward, fumbled with the door, flung it open and ran out into the reverberating rain. Then Gale followed him to the open door and shouted something after him. For most of the company, I think, it was lost in the din; but even if they had heard it, they certainly could not have understood it. I heard it; and I thought I understood it only too well. For what Gale shouted through the storm was, 'Why don't you call the chairs and they'll come to you.'

"A second or so afterwards he added, as if it were an afterthought, 'You might as well tell the tree to come here as well.' Naturally there was no answer; and indeed Saunders, partly by his natural clumsiness and partly in the distraction of the driving elements, seemed for the moment to have lost his way and was staggering up the steeper path of the meadow some way to the left of the tree. I could just see his long figure and angular awkward elbows traced against the sky. Then followed the sudden, violent and utterly unintelligible incident. A rope happened to lie half round one of the swathes in the foreground; and Gale, leaping out of the door, caught it up and seemed to be knotting it in a sort of savage haste. The next moment there swept across the sky the great swirling curves of a noose thrown in the manner of a lasso. And I could see the wavering figure on the dark ridge alter its attitude and rear up as against an invisible obstacle, as the rope tightened and tugged it back.

"I looked round for assistance; and was surprised and somewhat alarmed to find I was alone. The host and hostess, and the others, having despatched the obliging Saunders after the chairs, had rushed off to summon the servants or secure other doors and windows, or look after other fittings threatened by the weather; and there was no one but myself to watch the unmeaning and apparently imbecile tragedy outside. I saw Gale drag Saunders like a sack at the end of a rope along the whole length of windows and disappear round a corner of the house. But I turned cold with a new fear when, even as he rushed past, he snatched the hay-fork from the mound and seemed to disappear brandishing it, like the fabulous fork of a demon. I rushed after them, but slipping on the wet stones, hurt my foot and had to limp; the raving storm seemed to have swallowed up that lunatic and all his antics; and it was not until some time afterwards that men found how that dance had ended. Herbert Saunders was found tied to a tree, still alive and even unwounded, but presenting the appearance of having barely missed a murderous attack; for the prongs of the pitchfork were driven by sheer fury into the tree on each side of his neck, holding him pinned there as by an iron ring. Gabriel Gale was not found for nearly a day, until after the storm was spent and the sunshine had returned; and he was loitering about in an adjoining meadow blowing the clocks off dandelions. I have seldom known him so serene."

There was a short silence. "How is the other fellow – Saunders?" asked Butterworth, after a pause of frowning consideration. "Was he much hurt?"

"Had a shock and is still shaky, of course," answered Garth. "Had to go for a rest-cure or something; but I believe he's all right now. Only you can hardly expect a harmless person who's been half murdered in a raving attack like that to feel very friendly or forgiving. So I'm afraid they will make it a case of attempted murder unless we can get our friend off on medical grounds. As a matter of fact, I have him waiting outside in the car."

"Very well," said the London doctor, rising with abrupt composure and buttoning up his coat. "We had better go along to see him now and get it over."

The interview between Gale and the two doctors, at an adjacent hotel, was so short and so extraordinary that they went away with their very level heads turning like windmills. For Gale displayed nothing even of the merely childish innocence of levity attributed to him in the tale of the dandelions. He listened with patience, and a humorous and benevolent mildness which made the two doctors, who were considerably his seniors, feel as if they were being treated as juniors. When Garth began to break it to him gently that some sort of rest-cure was required in his own interests, he laughed heartily and anticipated all such periphrases.

"Don't be nervous, old man," he said, "you mean I ought to be in a madhouse; and I'm sure you mean well."

"You know I am your friend," said Garth earnestly; "and all your friends would say what I say."

"Indeed," said Gale, smiling. "Well, if that is the opinion of my friends, perhaps it would be better to get the opinion of my enemies."

"What do you mean," demanded the other. "Of your enemies?"

"Shall we say of my enemy?" continued Gale in level tones. "Of the man to whom I have done this perfectly outrageous thing. Well, really, that is all I ask; that before you lock me up for this outrage, you ask Herbert Saunders himself what he thinks about it."

"Do you mean," broke in Butterworth rather impatiently, "that we are to ask him whether he liked being half-throttled and impaled on a pitchfork?"

"Yes," said Gale nodding, "I want you to ask him whether he liked being half-throttled and impaled on a pitchfork."

He slightly knitted his brows as if considering a new and merely practical point and then added:

"I should send him a telegram now…say anything… 'How do you like being lassoed?' or, 'What price pitchforks?' or something playful of that sort."

"We could telephone, if it comes to that," said Garth.

The poet shook his head. "No," he said, "that sort of man feels much more free in writing. He will only stammer on the telephone. He won't stammer anything like what you imagine, even then; but he will stammer. But writing with his head in one of those little cubicles at the telegraph office, he will feel as free as in a confessional box."

The two doctors, when they parted in some bewilderment, but tacitly accepting this suggestion of a respite, lost no time in fulfilling the condition required. They sent off a carefully worded telegram to Saunders, who had now returned home to his mother's house, asking him what were his impressions and views about the extraordinary conduct of Gabriel Gale. The reply came back with remarkable promptitude; and Garth came to Butterworth with the open telegram in his hand and a rather dazed expression on his face. For the exact terms of the message were: "Can never be sufficiently grateful to Gale for his great kindness which more than saved my life."

The two doctors looked at each other in silence; and in almost as complete a silence got into a car and drove across the hills once more to the Blakeney's house, where Gale was still staying.

They drove across the hilly country and descended into the wide and shallow valley where stood the house which sheltered that dangerous character, Mr Gabriel Gale. Garth could recall, and Butterworth could imagine, all the irony suggested to the imagination by such a story about such a scene. The house of the Blakeneys stood high and plain just beyond the river; it was one of those houses that strike the eye as old-fashioned and yet not old. Certainly it was not old enough to be beautiful; but it had everything that recalls, to those that faintly remember them, the last traditions of Early Victorian lingering into Mid-Victorian times. The tall pillars looked so very pallid; the long plain windows looked in dismally upon high-ceilinged rooms; the curtains that hung parallel with the pillars were strips of dull red; and even from that distance the humorous Butterworth was certain that they had heavy and quite useless tassels. It was a strange house to have been the scene of an incredible crime or lunacy. It was an even stranger house to have been, as was alleged, the scene of a yet more incredible or mysterious mercy. All about it lay its ordered gardens and its mown or unmown meadows; its plantations of trees and deep alleys and shrubberies; all the things which on that wild night had been given over to the withering splendour of the lightning and the wind. Now the whole landscape was laid bare in a golden calm of summer; and the blue heavens above it were so deep and still that the sound of a humming fly hung there and was heard as far away as the skylark. Thus glittered in the sun, all solid and objective, the stage properties of that hideous farce. Garth saw all the blank and staring windows which he had last beheld streaming with rain and swept by the wind and the wild dance of the lunatic and his victim. He saw the forked tree to which the victim had been bound, still with the two black holes in it where the fork had pierced it, looking like the hollow eyes of a skull, and making the whole seem like some horned goblin. There was the heaped up hay, still to some extent disordered and scattered as by the dizzy dance of a small cyclone; and beyond it rose the high green wall of the unmown and standing grass of the next meadow. From the very thick of this mild jungle or miniature forest, a long thin line of smoke was drawn up into the sky; as if from a very small fire of weeds. Nothing else human or alive was visible in the sultry summer landscape; but Garth seemed to know and recognize the significance of the smoke. He sent a far halloo across the fields, calling out, "Is that you, Gale?"

Two feet pointed skyward and two long legs upside down rose vertically out of the tall grass, just beyond the smoke; and waved to them like arms, as if according to a pre-concerted science of signalling. Then the legs seemed to give a leap and dive and the owner of the legs came the right side up and rose or surged slowly out of the depths of green, gazing across at them with a misty and benevolent expression. He was smoking a long thin cigar: the fire behind the smoke.

He received them and their news with no air of triumph, still less of surprise. Abandoning his grassy nest, he sat down with them on the garden chairs which had also played their part in the mystery; and only smiled a little as he handed back the telegram.

"Well," he said; "do you still think I am mad?"

"Well," said Butterworth, "I can't help wondering whether he is."

Gale leaned across, showing his first eagerness, and said, "He isn't. But he jolly nearly was."

Then he leaned slowly back again and stared abstractedly at a daisy on the lawn, almost as if he had forgotten their presence. When he spoke again it was in a clear but rather colourless tone, like a lecturer:

"A very large number of young men nearly go mad. But nearly all of them only nearly do it; and normally they recover the normal. You might almost say it's normal to have an abnormal period. It comes when there's a lack of adjustment in the scale of things outside and within. Lots of those boys, those big healthy schoolboys you hear about, who care for nothing but cricket or the tuck shop, are bursting with a secret and swelling morbidity. But in this young man it was rather symbolically expressed even in the look of him. It was like his growing out of his clothes, or being too big for his boots. The inside gets too big for the outside. He doesn't know how to relate the two things; and generally he doesn't relate them at all. In one way his own mind and self seem to be colossal and cosmic and everything outside them small or distant. In another way the world is much too big for him; and his thoughts are fragile things to be hidden away. There are any number of cases of that disproportionate secretiveness. You know how silent boys have been about incredible abuses in bad schools. Whether or no it's false to say a girl can't keep a secret, it's often really the ruin of a boy that he can keep a secret.

"Now in that dangerous time, there's a dreadfully dangerous moment; when the first connexion is made between the subjective and objective: the first real bridge between the brain and real things. It all depends what it is; because, while it confirms his self-consciousness, it may happen to confirm his self-deception. That young man had never really been noticed by anybody until Lady Flamborough happened to tell him that he had brought the bad weather. It came just at the moment when his whole sense of proportions and possibilities had gone wild. I think the first thing that made me suspect he was... By the way," added Gale abruptly, "what was it that made you first suspect *me* of being mad?"

"I think," said Garth slowly, "it was when you were staring out of the window at the storm."

"The storm? Was there a storm?" asked Gale vaguely. "Oh yes, now I come to think of it, there was."

"But, hang it all," replied the doctor, "what else could you have been staring out of the window at, except the storm?"

"I wasn't staring out of the window," answered Gale.

"Really, my dear fellow," remonstrated Dr Garth.

"I was staring at the window," said the poet. "I often stare at windows. So few people ever look at windows, unless they are stained glass windows. But glass is a very beautiful thing, like diamonds; and transparency is a sort of transcendental colour. Besides, in this case there was something else; and something far more awful and thrilling than a thunderstorm."

"Well, what *were* you looking at, that was more awful than a thunderstorm?"

"I was looking at two raindrops running down the pane," said Gale. "And so was Saunders."

Seeing the others staring at him he continued: "Oh yes, it's quite true; as the poet says," and he recited with great and unusual gravity:

" 'Little drops of water,
    Little grains of sand,
    Make the soul to stagger
    Till the stars can hardly stand.'

"Haven't I told you a thousand times," he continued with increasing earnestness and animation, "that I always find myself looking at some little thing, a stone or a starfish or what not, and that's the only way I can ever learn anything? But when I looked at Saunders, I saw his eyes were fixed on the same spot on the window-pane; and I shuddered from head to foot, for I knew I had guessed right. He was wearing a certain kind of unobtrusive smile.

"You know that incurable gamblers sometimes bet on a race between two raindrops. But there is this specially about the sport; that it is abstract and equal and gives one a sense of impartiality. If you bet on a dogfight, you may find you really sympathize with a Scotch terrier against an Irish terrier, or *vice versa*; you may like the look of a billiard player or even the colours of a jockey. Therefore the event may go *against* your sympathies; and you will realize your limitations. But in the case of those two crystal spheres hung in a void of transparency, there is something like the equal scales of an abstract justice; you feel that whichever wins might be the one you had chosen. You may easily, in a certain secret megalomania, persuade yourself it is the one you have chosen. It is easy to imagine oneself controlling things hung so evenly. That was when I said to him, to test whether I was following his train of thought, 'It makes you feel like God.' Did you think I was talking about the storm? Storm! Pooh! Why should a storm make a man think he's God? If he'd got any sense it might make him feel he wasn't. But I knew that Saunders was just at the delicate crisis, where he was half trying to believe he was. He was half trying to think he had really changed the weather and might change everything; and a game like that of the raindrops was just the thing to encourage him. He really felt as if he were Omnipotence looking at two falling stars: and he was the special providence in them.

"Remember that there is always something double about morbidity; the sound old popular phrase said the madman was 'beside himself.' There is a part of him encouraging itself to go mad; and a part that still doesn't quite believe in the mania. He would delight in easy self-deceptions, as in the raindrops. He would also subconsciously *avoid* tests too decisive. He would avoid *wanting* to want something incredible; as that a tree should dance. He would avoid it; partly for fear it should and partly for fear it shouldn't. And I was suddenly and furiously certain, with every cell of my brain, that he must stop himself instantly, violently, by telling the tree to dance; and finding it wouldn't.

"That was when I shouted to him to tell the chairs and the tree to move. I was certain that unless he learnt his human limitations sharply and instantly, something illimitable and inhuman would take hold of him in that very hour. He took no notice; he rushed out into the garden; he forgot all about the chairs; he ran up that steep meadow with a leap like that of a wild goat; and I knew he had broken loose from reality and was out of the world. He would go careering through waste places, with the storm within and without; and when he returned from that country walk he would never be the same again. He would leap and dance on that lonely road; he would be horribly happy; nothing would stop him. I was already resolved that something must stop him. It must be something abrupt, arresting, revealing the limit of real things; the throttling shock with which a thing comes to the end of its tether. Then I saw the rope and threw it, catching him back like a wild horse. Somehow there rose in my imagination the image of the pagan Centaur rearing backwards, bridled, and rampant against heaven: for the Centaur, like all paganism, is at once natural and unnatural; a part of nature-worship and yet a monster.

"I went through with the whole wild business; and I was sure I was right; as he himself is now sure I was right. Nobody knew but I how far he had already gone along that road; and I knew that there was nothing for it but acute, practical, painful discovery that he could not control matter or the elements; that he could not move trees or remove pitchforks; that he could struggle for two hours with a rope and a pair of prongs and still be bound.

"It was certainly rather a desperate remedy; there is really nothing to be said for it except that it was a remedy. And I believe profoundly that there was no other remedy. Anything in the nature of soothing or quieting him would only have made him yet more secretive and yet more swollen-headed. As for humouring him, it's the very worst thing to do with people who are losing their sense of humour. No; there was something he was beginning to believe about himself; and it was still possible to prove that it wasn't true."

"Do you think," asked Dr Butterworth, frowning, "that there was really anything in that theological imagery in the matter? Do you suppose *he* put it in the form that he could bring the rain and thunder because he was God Almighty? Of course there are cases of religious mania that are rather like that."

"You must remember," said Gale, "that he was a theological student and was going to be a clergyman; and he may have brooded upon doubt and inspiration and prophecy till they began to work the wrong way. The worst is always very near the best; there is something much worse than atheism which is Satanism; otherwise known as Being God. But as a matter of mere philosophy, apart from theology, the thing is much nearer to the nerve of all thinking than you might think. That's why it was so insinuating and so difficult to see or to stop. That's what I mean when I say I had a sympathy with the young lunatic. After all, it was a very natural mistake."

"My dear Gale," protested his friend Garth. "You are getting a little too fond of paradox. A young tadpole of a curate thinks he can control the skies and uproot trees and call up the thunder and you call it a natural mistake."

"Have you ever lain on your back in a field and stared at the sky and kicked your heels in the air?" asked the poet.

"Not in a public or professional way," answered the doctor. "It's not generally considered the best bedside manner. But suppose I did?"

"If you think like that, and go back to primitive things," said Gale, "you will find yourself wondering why you can control some things and not others. After all, your legs look a long way off when you wave them in the sky. You can wave legs about, but you can't wave trees about. I'm not sure it's so unnatural, in the abstract, for a man to fancy the whole material universe is his own body; since it all seems equally, in one sense, to be outside his own mind. But when he is in hell is when he fancies it is inside his own mind."

"I'm afraid I don't bother much about all this metaphysical business," said Butterworth. "I suppose I really don't understand it. I know what I mean by a man being outside his mind in the sense of being out of his mind; and I suppose you're right in saying that Saunders was morbid enough to be nearly out of his mind. And as for being outside his body, I know what it means in the sense of his blowing his brains out or his body being left for dead. And really, to be candid, you seem to have come precious near to knocking him out of his body to cure him of being out of his mind. It certainly was an exceedingly desperate remedy; and though it may have been defensible, I shouldn't much like to have to go into a law court as an expert witness to defend it. I can only go by results, and he certainly seems to be all the better for it. But when it comes to all your mystical explanations, about how it is hell to have everything inside your mind, frankly I give up trying to follow. I'm afraid I'm rather a materialist."

"Afraid!" cried Gale, as if with indignation; "*afraid* you are a materialist! You haven't got much notion of what there really is to be afraid of! Materialists are all right; they are at least near enough to heaven to accept the earth and not imagine they made it. The dreadful doubts are not the doubts of the materialist. The dreadful doubts, the deadly and damnable doubts, are the doubts of the idealist."

"I always imagined you were an idealist," said Garth.

"I use the word idealist in its philosophical sense. I mean the real sceptic who doubts matter and the minds of others and everything except his own ego. I have been through it myself; as I have been through nearly every form of infernal idiocy. That is the only use I am in the world; having been every kind of idiot. But believe me, the worst and most miserable sort of idiot is he who seems to create and contain all things. Man is a creature; all his happiness consists in being a creature; or, as the Great Voice commanded us, in becoming a child. All his fun is in having a gift or present; which the child, with profound understanding, values because it is 'a surprise'. But surprise implies that a thing came from outside ourselves; and gratitude that it comes from someone other than ourselves. It is thrust through the letterbox; it is thrown in at the window; it is thrown over the wall. Those limits are the lines of the very plan of human pleasure.

"I also dreamed that I had dreamed of the whole creation. I had given myself the stars for a gift; I had handed myself the sun and moon. I had been behind and at the beginning of all things; and without me nothing was made that was made. Anybody who has been in that centre of the cosmos knows that it is to be in hell. And there is only one cure for it. Oh, I know that people have written all kinds of cant and false comfort about the cause of evil; and of why there is pain in the world. God forbid that we should add ourselves to such a chattering monkey-house of moralists. But for all that, this truth is true; objectively and experimentally true. There is no cure for that nightmare of omnipotence except pain; because that is the thing a man *knows* he would not tolerate if he could really control it. A man must be in some place from which he would certainly escape if he could, if he is really to realize that all things do not come from within. That is the meaning of that mad parable or mystery play you have seen acted here like an allegory. I doubt whether any of our action is really anything but an allegory. I doubt whether any truth can be told except in a parable. There was a man who saw himself sitting in the sky; and his servants the angels went to and fro in coloured garments of cloud and flame and the pageant of the seasons; but he was over all and his face seemed to fill the heavens. And, God forgive me for blasphemy, but I nailed him to a tree."

He had risen to his feet in a suppressed and very unusual excitement; and his face was pale in the sunlight. For he spoke indeed in parables; and the things of which he was thinking were far away from that garden or even from that tale. There swelled up darkly and mountainously in his memory the slopes of another garden against another storm. The skeleton arch of a ruined abbey stood gaunt against the ghastly light, and beyond the racing river was the low and desolate inn among the reeds; and all that grey landscape was to him one purple patch of Paradise – and of Paradise Lost.

"It is the only way," he kept repeating; "it is the only answer to the heresy of the mystic; which is to fancy that mind is all. It is to break your heart. Thank God for hard stones; thank God for hard facts; thank God for thorns and rocks and deserts and long years. At least I know now that I am not the best or strongest thing in the world. At least I know now that I have not dreamed of everything."

"You look very strange," said his friend Garth.

"I know it now," said Gale. "For there is one who would be here, if dreaming could do it."

There was again an utter stillness in which the fly could be heard buzzing in the blue; and when he spoke again, though in the same brooding vein, they had an indescribable intuition that a door in his mind had stood open for an instant and had now again closed finally with a clang. He said after the long silence: "We are all tied to trees and pinned with pitchforks. And as long as these are solid we know the stars will stand and the hills will not melt at our word. Can't you imagine the huge tide of healthy relief and thanks, like a hymn of praise from all nature, that went up from that captive nailed to the tree, when he had wrestled till the dawn and received at last the great and glorious news; the news that he was only a man?"

Dr Butterworth was looking across the table with a restrained but somewhat amused expression; for the poet's eyes were shining like lamps and he was speaking on a note not often heard in any man speaking prose.

"If I hadn't got a good deal of special knowledge and experience," he said, rising, "I should think there was a bit of a doubt about you after all."

Gabriel Gale looked sharply over his shoulder and the note of his voice changed once more.

"Don't say that," he said rather curtly. "That's the only sort of danger I really run."

"I don't understand," said Butterworth. "Do you mean the danger of being certified?"

"Certify me till all is blue," said Gale contemptuously. "Do you suppose I should particularly mind if you did? Do you suppose I couldn't be reasonably happy in a lunatic asylum, so long as there was dust in a sunbeam or shadows on a wall – so long as I could look at ordinary things and think how extraordinary they are? Do you suppose I couldn't praise God with tolerable piety for the shape of my keeper's nose or anything else calculated to give pleasure to a thoughtful mind? I should imagine that a madhouse would be an excellent place to be sane in. I'd a long sight rather live in a nice quiet secluded madhouse than in intellectual clubs full of unintellectual people, all chattering nonsense about the newest book of philosophy; or in some of those earnest, elbowing sort of Movements that want you to go in for Service and help to take away somebody else's toys. I don't much mind to what place I may wander to think in, before I die; so long as the thoughts do not wander too much; or wander down the wrong road. And what you said just now does touch the real danger. It does touch the danger that Garth was really thinking about, when he suggested that I had reclaimed lunatics and might myself become a castaway. If people tell me they really do not understand what I mean – if they say they cannot see so simple a truth as that it is best for a man to be a man, that it is dangerous to give oneself divine honours – if they say they do not see *that* for themselves, but imagine it to be some sort of mysticism out of my own head, *then* I am myself again in peril. I am in peril of thinking something that may be wilder and worse than thinking I am God Almighty."

"And still I don't understand," said the smiling physician.

"I shall think I am the only sane man," said Gabriel Gale.

There was a sort of sequel which came to Garth's ears long afterwards; an epilogue to the crazy comedy of the pitchfork and the apple tree. Garth differed from Gale in having a more obvious turn for the rational, or at least the rationalistic; and he often found himself debating with the sceptics of various scientific clubs and groups; finding them a very worthy race, often genuinely hard-headed and sometimes tending rather to be wooden-headed. In a particular country place, the name of which is not material, the post of village atheist had become vacant, so to speak, by the regrettable perversity of the cobbler in being a Congregationalist. His official functions were performed by a more prosperous person named Pond, a worthy hatter who was rather more famous as a cricketer. On the cricket field he was often pitted against another excellent cricketer, who was Vicar of the parish; indeed they contended more frequently on the field of cricket than on the field of spiritual speculation. For the clergyman was one of the type that is uproariously popular and successful chiefly by his proficiency in such sports. He was the sort of parson whom people praise by saying he is not a bit like a parson. He was a big, beefy, jolly man, red-faced and resolute of manner; still young but the father of a boisterous family of boys, and in most ways very like a boy himself. Nevertheless, as was natural, certain passages of chaff, that could hardly be called controversy, occasionally passed between the parson and the village atheist. There was no need to commiserate the clergyman upon the pinpricks of the scientific materialist; for a pin has no effect on a pachyderm. The parson was the sort of man who seems to be rolled in layers within layers of solid substance resisting anything outside his own cheery and sensible mode of life. But one curious episode had clung to the memory of Pond, and he recounted it to Garth, in something of the puzzled tone in which a materialist tells a ghost story. The rival cricketers had been chipping each other in the usual friendly fashion, which did not go very much below the surface. The Vicar was doubtless a sincere Christian, though chiefly what used to be called a muscular Christian. But it is not unfair to him to say that he was more deeply moved in saying that some action was not Cricket than in saying it was not Christianity. On this and other occasions, however, he relied chiefly on ragging his opponent with rather obvious jokes; such as the oft-repeated inquiry as to how often the hatter might be expected to do the hat-trick. Perhaps the repetition of this epigram eventually annoyed the worthy freethinker; or perhaps there was something in the deeper and more positive tones with which the parson dealt with more serious matters, that had the same effect. It was with more than his usual breeziness that the reverend gentleman on this occasion affirmed the philosophy of his life. "God wants you to play the game," he said. "That's all that God wants; people who will play the game."

"How do you know?" asked Mr Pond rather snappishly and in unusual irritation. "How do you know what God wants? You never were God, were you?"

There was a silence; and the atheist was seen to be staring at the red face of the parson in a somewhat unusual fashion.

"Yes," said the clergyman in a queer quiet voice. "I was God once; for about fourteen hours. But I gave it up. I found it was too much of a strain."

With these words the Rev. Herbert Saunders went back to the cricket tent, where he mingled with Boy Scouts and village girls with all his usual heartiness and hilarity. But Mr Pond the atheist, sat for some time staring, like one who has seen a miracle. And he afterwards confided to Garth that for a moment the eyes of Saunders had looked out of his red, good-humoured face as out of a mask; with an instantaneous memory of something awful and appalling, and at the same time empty; something the other man could only figure to himself in vague thoughts of some flat stark building with blank windows in a blind alley; and peering out of one of the windows the pale face of an idiot.

V

THE FINGER OF STONE

Three young men on a walking tour came to a halt outside the little town of Carillon, in the south of France; which is doubtless described in the guide books as famous for its fine old Byzantine monastery, now the seat of a university; and for having been the scene of the labours of Boyg. At that name, at least, the reader will be reasonably thrilled; for he must have seen it in any number of newspapers and novels. Boyg and the Bible are periodically reconciled at religious conferences; Boyg broadens and slightly bewilders the minds of numberless heroes of long psychological stories, which begin in the nursery and nearly end in the madhouse. The journalist, writing rapidly his recurrent reference to the treatment meted out to pioneers like Galileo, pauses in the effort to think of another example, and always rounds off the sentence either with Bruno or with Boyg. But the mildly orthodox are equally fascinated, and feel a glow of agnosticism while they continue to say that, since the discoveries of Boyg, the doctrine of the Homoousian or of the human conscience does not stand where it did; wherever that was. It is needless to say that Boyg was a great discoverer, for the public has long regarded him with the warmest reverence and gratitude on that ground. It is also unnecessary to say what he discovered; for the public will never display the faintest curiosity about that. It is vaguely understood that it was something about fossils, or the long period required for petri-faction; and that it generally implied those anarchic or anonymous forces of evolution supposed to be hostile to religion. But certainly none of the discoveries he made while he was alive was so sensational, in the newspaper sense, as the discovery that was made about him when he was dead. And this, the more private and personal matter, is what concerns us here.

The three tourists had just agreed to separate for an hour, and meet again for luncheon at the little café, opposite; and the different ways in which they occupied their time and indulged their tastes will serve for a sufficient working summary of their personalities. Arthur Armitage was a dark and grave young man, with a great deal of money, which he spent on a conscientious and continuous course of self-culture, especially in the matter of art and architecture; and his earnest aquiline profile was already set towards the Byzantine monastery, for the exhaustive examination of which he had already prepared himself, as if he were going to pass an examination rather than to make one. The man next to him, though himself an artist, betrayed no such artistic ardour. He was a painter who wasted most of his time as a poet; but Armitage, who was always picking up geniuses, had become in some sense his patron in both departments. His name was Gabriel Gale; a long, loose, rather listless man with yellow hair; but a man not easy for any patron to patronize.

He generally did as he liked in an abstracted fashion; and what he very often liked to do was nothing. On this occasion he showed a lamentable disposition to drift towards the café first; and having drunk a glass or two of wine, he drifted not into the town but out of it, roaming about the steep bare slope above, with a rolling eye on the rolling clouds; and talking to himself until he found somebody else to talk to, which happened when he put his foot through the glass roof of a studio just below him on the steep incline. As it was an artist's studio, however, their quarrel fortunately ended in an argument about the future of realistic art; and when he turned up to lunch, that was the extent of his acquaintance with the quaint and historic town of Carillon.

The name of the third man was Garth; he was shorter and uglier and somewhat older than the others, but with a much livelier eye in his hatchet face; he stepped much more briskly, and in the matter of a knowledge of the world, the other two were babies under his charge. He was a very able medical practitioner, with a hobby of more fundamental scientific inquiry; and for him the whole town, university and studio, monastery and café was only the temple of the presiding genius of Boyg. But in this case the practical instinct of Dr Garth would seem to have guided him rightly; for he discovered things considerably more startling than anything the antiquarian found in the Romanesque arches or the poet in the rolling clouds. And it is his adventures, in that single hour before lunch, upon which this tale must turn.

The café tables stood on the pavement under a row of trees opposite the old round gate in the wall, through which could be seen the white gleam of the road up which they had just been walking. But the steep hills were so high round the town that they rose clear above the wall, in a more enormous wall of smooth and slanting rock, bare except for occasional clumps of cactus. There was no crack in that sloping wilderness of stone except the rather shallow and stony bed of a little stream. Lower down, where the stream reached the level of the valley, rose the dark domes of the basilica of the old monastery; and from this a curious stairway of rude stones ran some way up the hill beside the watercourse, and stopped at a small and solitary building looking little more than a shed made of stones. Some little way higher the gleam of the glass roof of the studio, with which Gale had collided in his unconscious wanderings, marked the last spot of human habitation in all those rocky wastes that rose about the little town.

Armitage and Gale were already seated at the table when Dr Garth walked up briskly and sat down somewhat abruptly.

"Have you fellows heard the news?" he asked.

He spoke somewhat sharply, for he was faintly annoyed by the attitudes of the antiquarian and the artist, who were deep in their own dreamier and less practical tastes and topics. Armitage was saying at the moment:

"Yes, I suppose I've seen today some of the very oldest sculpture of the veritable Dark Ages. And it's not stiff like some Byzantine work; there's a touch of the true grotesque you generally get in Gothic."

"Well, I've seen today some of the newest sculpture of the Modern Ages," replied Gale, "and I fancy they are the veritable Dark Ages. Quite enough of the true grotesque up in that studio, I can tell you."

"Have you heard the news, I say?" rapped out the doctor. "Boyg is dead."

Gale stopped in a sentence about Gothic architecture, and said seriously, with a sort of hazy reverence: "*Requiescat in pace.* Who was Boyg?"

"Well, really," replied the doctor, "I did think every baby had heard of Boyg."

"Well, I dare say you've never heard of Paradou," answered Gale. "Each of us lives in his little cosmos with its classes and degrees. Probably you haven't heard of the most advanced sculptor, or perhaps of the latest lacrosse expert or champion chess player."

It was characteristic of the two men, that while Gale went on talking in the air about an abstract subject, till he had finished his own train of thought, Armitage had a sufficient proper sense of the presence of something more urgent to relapse into silence. Nevertheless, he unconsciously looked down at his notes; at the name of the advanced sculptor he looked up.

"Who is Paradou?" he asked.

"Why, the man I've been talking to this morning," replied Gale. "His sculpture's advanced enough for anybody. He's no end of a chap; talks more than I do, and talks very well. Thinks too; I should think he could do everything except sculpt. There his theories get in his way. As I told him, this notion of the new realism – "

"Perhaps we might drop realism and attend to reality," said Dr Garth grimly. "I tell you Boyg is dead. And that's not the worst either."

Armitage looked up from his notes with something of the vagueness of his friend the poet. "If I remember right," he said, "Professor Boyg's discovery was concerned with fossils."

"Professor Boyg's discovery involved the extension of the period required for petrifaction as distinct from fossilization," replied the doctor stiffly, "and thereby relegated biological origins to a period which permits the chronology necessary to the hypothesis of natural selection. It may affect you as humorous to interject the observation 'loud cheers', but I assure you the scientific world, which happens to be competent to judge, was really moved with amazement as well as admiration."

"In fact it was petrified to hear it couldn't be petrified," suggested the poet.

"I have really no time for your flippancy," said Garth. "I am up against a great ugly fact."

Armitage interposed in the benevolent manner of a chairman. "We must really let Garth speak; come, doctor, what is it all about? Begin at the beginning."

"Very well," said the doctor, in his staccato way. "I'll begin at the beginning. I came to this town with a letter of introduction to Boyg himself; and as I particularly wanted to visit the geological museum, which his own munificence provided for this town, I went there first. I found all the windows of the Boyg Museum were broken; and the stones thrown by the rioters were actually lying about the room within a foot or two of the glass cases, one of which was smashed."

"Donations to the geological museum, no doubt," remarked Gale. "A munificent patron happens to pass by, and just heaves in a valuable exhibit through the window. I don't see why that shouldn't be done in what you call the world of science; I'm sure it's done all right in the world of art. Old Paradou's busts and bas-reliefs are just great rocks chucked at the public and – "

"Paradou may go to – Paradise, shall we say?" said Garth, with pardonable impatience. "Will nothing make you understand that something has really happened that isn't any of your ideas and isms? It wasn't only the geological museum; it was the same everywhere. I passed by the house Boyg first lived in, where they very properly put up a medallion; and the medallion was all splashed with mud. I crossed the market-place, where they put up a statue to him just recently. It was still hung with wreaths of laurel by his pupils and the party that appreciates him; but they were half torn away, as if there had been a struggle, and stones had evidently been thrown, for a piece of the hand was chipped off."

"Paradou's statue, no doubt," observed Gale. "No wonder they threw things at it."

"I think not," replied the doctor, in the same hard voice. "It wasn't because it was Paradou's statue, but because it was Boyg's statue. It was the same business as the museum and the medallion. No, there's been something like a French Revolution here on the subject; the French are like that. You remember the riot in the Breton village where Renan was born, against having a statue of him. You know, I suppose, that Boyg was a Norwegian by birth, and only settled here because the geological formation, and the supposed mineral properties of that stream there, offered the best field for his investigations. Well, besides the fits the parsons were in at his theories in general, it seems he bumped into some barbarous local superstition as well; about it being a sacred stream that froze snakes into ammonites at a wink; a common myth, of course, for the same was told about St Hilda at Whitby. But there are peculiar conditions that made it pretty hot in this place. The theological students fight with the medical students, one for Rome and the other for Reason; and they say there's a sort of raving lunatic of a Peter the Hermit, who lives in that hermitage on the hill over there, and every now and then comes out waving his arms and setting the place on fire."

"I heard something about that," remarked Armitage. "The priest who showed me over the monastery; I think he was the head man there – anyhow, he was a most learned and eloquent gentleman – told me about a holy man on the hill who was almost canonized already."

"One is tempted to wish he were martyred already; but the martyrdom, if any, was not his," said Garth darkly. "Allow me to continue my story in order. I had crossed the market-place to find Professor Boyg's private house, which stood at the corner of it. I found the shutters up and the house apparently empty, except for one old servant, who refused at first to tell me anything; indeed, I found a good deal of rustic reluctance on both sides to tell a foreigner anything. But when I had managed to make the nature of my introduction quite plain to him, he finally broke down; and told me his master was dead."

There was a pause, and then Gale, who seemed for the first time somewhat impressed, asked abstractedly: "Where is his tomb? Your tale is really rather strange and dramatic, and obviously it must go on to his tomb. Your pilgrimage ought to end in finding a magnificent monument of marble and gold, like the tomb of Napoleon, and then finding that even the grave had been desecrated."

"He has no tomb," replied Garth sternly, "though he will have many monuments. I hope to see the day when he will have a statue in every town, he whose statue is now insulted in his own town. But he will have no tomb."

"And why not?" asked the staring Armitage.

"His body cannot be found," answered the doctor; "no trace of him can be found anywhere."

"Then how do you know he is dead?" asked the other.

There was an instant of silence, and then the doctor spoke out in a voice fuller and stronger than before:

"Why, as to that," he said, "I think he is dead because I am sure he is murdered."

Armitage shut his notebook, but continued to look down steadily at the table. "Go on with your story," he said.

"Boyg's old servant," resumed the doctor, "who is a queer, silent, yellow-faced old card, was at last induced to tell me of the existence of Boyg's assistant, of whom I think he was rather jealous. The Professor's scientific helper and right-hand man is a man of the name of Bertrand, and a very able man, too, eminently worthy of the great man's confidence, and intensely devoted to his cause. He is carrying on Boyg's work so far as it can be carried on; and about Boyg's death or disappearance he knows the little that can be known. It was when I finally ran him to earth in a little house full of Boyg's books and instruments, at the bottom of the hill just beyond the town, that I first began to realize the nature of this sinister and mysterious business. Bertrand is a quiet man, though he has a little of the pardonable vanity which is not uncommon in assistants. One would sometimes fancy the great discovery was almost as much his as his master's; but that does no harm, since it only makes him fight for his master's fame almost as if it were his. But in fact he is not only concerned about the discovery; or rather, he is not only concerned about that discovery. I had not looked for long at the dark bright eyes and keen face of that quiet young man before I realized that there was something else that he is trying to discover. As a matter of fact, he is no longer merely a scientific assistant, or even a scientific student. Unless I am much mistaken, he is playing the part of an amateur detective.

"Your artistic training, my friends, may be an excellent thing for discovering a poet, or even a sculptor; but you will forgive me for thinking a scientific training rather better for discovering a murderer. Bertrand has gone to work in a very workmanlike way, I consider, and I can tell you in outline what he has discovered so far. Boyg was last seen by Bertrand descending the hillside by the water-course, having just come away from the studio of Gale's friend the sculptor, where he was sitting for an hour every morning. I may say here, rather for the sake of logical method than because it is needed by the logical argument; that the sculptor at any rate had no quarrel with Boyg, but was, on the contrary, an ardent admirer of him as an advanced and revolutionary character."

"I know," said Gale, seeming to take his head suddenly out of the clouds. "Paradou says realistic art must be founded on the modern energy of science; but the fallacy of that – "

"Let me finish with the facts first before you retire into your theories," said the doctor firmly. "Bertrand saw Boyg sit down on the bare hillside for a smoke; and you can see from here how bare a hillside it is; a man walking for hours on it would still be as visible as a fly crawling on a ceiling. Bertrand says he was called away to the crisis of an experiment in the laboratory; when he looked again he could not see his master, and he has never seen him from that day to this.

"At the foot of the hill, and at the bottom of the flight of steps which runs up to the hermitage, is the entrance to the great monastic buildings on the very edge of the town. The very first thing you come to on that side is the great quadrangle, which is enclosed by cloisters, and by the rooms or cells of the clerical or semi-clerical students. I need not trouble you with the tale of the political compromise by which this part of the institution has remained clerical, while the scientific and other schools beyond it are now entirely secular. But it is important to fix in your mind the fact itself: that the monastic part is on the very edge of the town, and the other part bars its way, so to speak, to the inside of the town. Boyg could not possibly have gone past that secular barrier, dead or alive, without being under the eyes of crowds who were more excited about him than about anything else in the world. For the whole place was in a fuss, and even a riot for him as well as against him. Something happened to him on the hillside, or anyhow before he came to the internal barrier. My friend the amateur detective set to work to examine the hillside, or all of it that could seriously count; an enormous undertaking, but he did it as if with a microscope. Well, he found that rocky field, when examined closely, very much what it looks even from here. There are no caves or even holes, there are no chasms or even cracks in that surface of blank stone for miles and miles. A rat could not be hidden in those few tufts of prickly pear. He could not find a hiding place; but for all that, he found a hint. The hint was nothing more than a faded scrap of paper, damp and draggled from the shallow bed of the brook, but faintly decipherable on it were words in the writing of the Master. They were but part of a sentence, but they included the words, 'will call on you tomorrow to tell you something you ought to know.'

"My friend Bertrand sat down and thought it out. The letter had been in the water, so it had not been thrown away in the town, for the highly scientific reason that the river does not flow uphill. There only remained on the higher ground the sculptor's studio and the hermitage. But Boyg would not write to the sculptor to warn him that he was going to call, since he went to his studio every morning. Presumably the person he was going to call on was the hermit; and a guess might well be made about the nature of what he had to say. Bertrand knew better than anybody that Boyg had just brought his great discovery to a crushing completeness, with fresh facts and ratifications; and it seems likely enough that he went to announce it to his most fanatical opponent, to warn him to give up the struggle."

Gale, who was gazing up into the sky with his eye on a bird, again abruptly intervened.

"In these attacks on Boyg," he said, "were there any attacks on his private character?"

"Even these madmen couldn't attack that," replied Garth with some heat. "He was the best sort of Scandinavian, as simple as a child, and I really believe as innocent. But they hated him for all that; and you can see for yourself that their hatred begins to appear on the horizon of our inquiry. He went to tell the truth in the hour of triumph; and he never reappeared to the light of the sun."

Armitage's far-away gaze was fixed on the solitary cell half-way up the hill. "You don't mean seriously," he said, "that the man they talk about as a saint, the friend of my friend the abbot, or whatever he is, is neither more nor less than an assassin?"

"You talked to your friend the abbot about Romanesque sculpture," replied Garth. "If you had talked to him about fossils, you might have seen another side to his character. These Latin priests are often polished enough, but you bet they're pointed as well. As for the other man on the hill, he's allowed by his superiors to live what they call the eremitical life; but he's jolly well allowed to do other things, too. On great occasions he's allowed to come down here and preach, and I can tell you there is Bedlam let loose when he does. I might be ready to excuse the man as a sort of a maniac; but I haven't the slightest difficulty in believing that he is a homicidal maniac."

"Did your friend Bertrand take any legal steps on his suspicions?" asked Armitage, after a pause.

"Ah, that's where the mystery begins," replied the doctor.

After a moment of frowning silence, he resumed. "Yes, he did make a formal charge to the police, and the Juge d'Instruction examined a good many people and so on, and said the charge had broken down. It broke down over the difficulty of disposing of the body; the chief difficulty in most murders. Now the hermit, who is called Hyacinth, I believe, was summoned in due course; but he had no difficulty in showing that his hermitage was as bare and as hard as the hillside. It seemed as if nobody could possibly have concealed a corpse in those stone walls, or dug a grave in that rocky floor. Then it was the turn of the abbot, as you call him, Father Bernard of the Catholic College. And he managed to convince the magistrate that the same was true of the cells surrounding the college quadrangle, and all the other rooms under his control. They were all like empty boxes, with barely a stick or two of furniture; less than usual, in fact, for some of the sticks had been broken up for the bonfire demonstration I told you of. Anyhow, that was the line of defence, and I dare say it was well conducted, for Bernard is a very able man, and knows about many other things besides Romanesque architecture; and Hyacinth, fanatic as he is, is famous as a persuasive orator. Anyhow, it was successful, the case broke down; but I am sure my friend Bertrand is only biding his time, and means to bring it up again. These difficulties about the concealment of a corpse – Hullo! why here he is in person."

He broke off in surprise as a young man walking rapidly down the street paused a moment, and then approached the café table at which they sat. He was dressed with all the funereal French respectability: his black stove-pipe hat, his high and stiff black neck cloth resembling a stock, and the curious corners of dark beard at the edges of his chin, gave him an antiquated air like a character out of Gaboriau. But if he was out of Gaboriau, he was nobody less than Lecocq; the dark eyes in his pale face might indeed be called the eyes of a born detective. At this moment, the pale face was paler than usual with excitement, and as he stopped a moment behind the doctor's chair, he said to him in a low voice: "I have found out."

Dr Garth sprang to his feet, his eyes brilliant with curiosity; then, recovering his conventional manner, he presented M. Bertrand to his friends, saying to the former, "You may speak freely with us, I think; we have no interest except an interest in the truth."

"I have found the truth," said the Frenchman, with compressed lips. "I know now what these murderous monks have done with the body of Boyg."

"Are we to be allowed to hear it?" asked Armitage gravely.

"Everyone will hear it in three days' time," replied the pale Frenchman. "As the authorities refuse to reopen the question, we are holding a public meeting in the market-place to demand that they do so. The assassins will be there, doubtless, and I shall not only denounce but convict them to their faces. Be there yourself, monsieur, on Thursday at half-past two, and you will learn how one of the world's greatest men was done to death by his enemies. For the moment I will only say one word. As the great Edgar Poe said in your own language, 'Truth is not always in a well.' I believe it is sometimes too obvious to be seen."

Gabriel Gale, who had rather the appearance of having gone to sleep, seemed to rouse himself with an unusual animation.

"That's true," he said, "and that's the truth about the whole business."

Armitage turned to him with an expression of quiet amusement.

"Surely you're not playing the detective, Gale," he said. "I never pictured such a thing as your coming out of fairyland to assist Scotland Yard."

"Perhaps Gale thinks he can find the body," suggested Dr Garth laughing.

Gale lifted himself slowly and loosely from his seat, and answered in his dazed fashion:

"Why, yes, in a way," he said; "in fact, I'm pretty sure I can find the body. In fact, in a manner of speaking, I've found it."

Those with any intimations of the personality of Mr Arthur Armitage will not need to be told that he kept a diary; and endeavoured to note down his impressions of foreign travel with atmospheric sympathy and the *mot juste*. But the pen dropped from his hand, so to speak, or at least wandered over the page in a mazy desperation, in the attempt to describe the great mob meeting, or rather the meeting of two mobs, which took place in the picturesque market-place in which he had wandered alone a few days before, criticising the style of the statue, or admiring the skyline of the basilica. He had read and written about democracy all his life; and when first he met it, it swallowed him like an earthquake. One actual and appalling difference divided this French mob in a provincial market from all the English mobs he had ever seen in Hyde Park or Trafalgar Square. These Frenchmen had not come there to get rid of their feelings, but to get rid of their enemies. Something would be done as a result of this sort of public meeting; it might be murder, but it would be something.

And although, or rather because, it had this militant ferocity, it had also a sort of military discipline. The clusters of men voluntarily deployed into cordons, and in some rough fashion followed the command of leaders. Father Bernard was there, with a face of bronze, like the mask of a Roman emperor, eagerly obeyed by his crowd of crusading devotees, and beside him the wild preacher, Hyacinth, who looked himself like a dead man brought out of the grave, with a face built out of bones, and cavernous eye-sockets deep and dark enough to hide the eyes. On the other side were the grim pallor of Bertrand and the rat-like activity of the red-haired Dr Garth; their own anti-clerical mob was roaring behind them, and their eyes were alight with triumph. Before Armitage could collect himself sufficiently to make proper notes of any of these things, Bertrand had sprung upon a chair placed near the pedestal of the statue, and announced almost without words, by one dramatic gesture, that he had come to avenge the dead.

Then the words came, and they came thick and fast, telling and terrible; but Armitage heard them as in a dream till they reached the point for which he was waiting; the point that would awaken any dreamer. He heard the prose poems of laudation, the hymn to Boyg the hero, the tale of his tragedy so far as he knew it already. He heard the official decision about the impossibility of the clerics concealing the corpse, as he had heard it already. And then he and the whole crowd leapt together at something they did not know before; or rather, as in all such riddles, something they did know and did not understand.

"They plead that their cells are bare and their lives simple," Bertrand was saying, "and it is true that these slaves of superstition are cut off from the natural joys of men. But they have their joys; oh, believe me, they have their festivities. If they cannot rejoice in love, they can rejoice in hatred. And everybody seems to have forgotten that on the very day the Master vanished, the theological students in their own quadrangle burnt him in effigy. In effigy."

A thrill that was hardly a whisper, but was wilder than a cry, went through the whole crowd; and men had taken in the whole meaning before they could keep pace with the words that followed.

"Did they burn Bruno in effigy? Did they burn Dolet in effigy?" Bertrand was saying, with a white, fanatical face. "Those martyrs of the truth were burned alive for the good of their Church and for the glory of their God. Oh, yes, progress has improved them; and they did not burn Boyg alive. But they burned him dead; and that is how they obliterated the traces of the way they had done him to death. I have said that truth is not always hidden in a well, but rather high on a tower. And while I have searched every crevice and cactus bush for the bones of my master, it was in truth in public, under the open sky, before a roaring crowd in the quadrangle, that his body vanished from the sight of men."

When the last cheer and howl of a whole hell of such noises had died away, Father Bernard succeeded in making his voice heard.

"It is enough to say in answer to this maniac charge that the atheists who bring it against us cannot induce their own atheistic Government to support them. But as the charge is against Father Hyacinth rather than against me, I will ask him to reply to it."

There was another tornado of conflicting noises when the eremitical preacher opened his mouth; but his very tones had a certain power of piercing, and quelling it. There was something strange in such a voice coming out of such a skull-and-cross-bones of a countenance; for it was unmistakably the musical and moving voice that had stirred so many congregations and pilgrimages. Only in this crisis it had an awful accent of reality, which was beyond any arts of oratory. But before the tumult had yet died away Armitage, moved by some odd nervous instinct, had turned abruptly to Garth and said, "What's become of Gale? He said he was going to be here. Didn't he talk some nonsense about bringing the body himself?"

Dr Garth shrugged his shoulders. "I imagine he's talking some other nonsense at the top of the hill somewhere else. You mustn't ask poets to remember all the nonsense they talk."

"My friends," Father Hyacinth was saying, in quiet but penetrating tones. "I have no answer to give to this charge. I have no proofs with which to refute it. If a man can be sent to the guillotine on such evidence, to the guillotine I will go. Do you fancy I do not know that innocent men have been guillotined? M. Bertrand spoke of the burning of Bruno, as if it is only the enemies of the Church that have been burned. Does any Frenchman forget that Joan of Arc was burned; and was she guilty? The first Christians were tortured for being cannibals, a charge as probable as the charge against me. Do you imagine because you kill men now by modern machinery and modern

107

law, that we do not know that you are as likely to kill unjustly as Herod or Heliogabalus? Do you think we do not know that the powers of the world are what they always were, that your lawyers who oppress the poor for hire will shed innocent blood for gold? If I were here to bandy such lawyer's talk, I could use it against you more reasonably than you against me. For what reason am I supposed to have imperilled my soul by such a monstrous crime? For a theory about a theory; for a hypothesis about a hypothesis, for some thin fantastic notion that a discovery about fossils threatened the everlasting truth. I could point to others who had better reasons for murder than that. I could point to a man who by the death of Boyg has inherited the whole power and position of Boyg. I could point to one who is truly the heir and the man whom the crime benefits; who is known to claim much of the discovery as his own; who has been not so much the assistant as the rival of the dead. He alone has given evidence that Boyg was seen on the hill at all on that fatal day. He alone inherits by the death anything solid, from the largest ambitions in the scientific world, to the smallest magnifying glass in his collection. The man lives, and I could stretch out my hand and touch him."

Hundreds of faces were turned upon Bertrand with a frightful expression of inhuman eagerness; the turn of the debate had been too dramatic to raise a cry. Bertrand's very lips were pale, but they smiled as they formed the words:

"And what did I do with the body?"

"God grant you did nothing with it, dead or alive," answered the other. "I do not charge you; but if ever you are charged as I am unjustly, you may need a God on that day. Though I were ten times guillotined, God could testify to my innocence; if it were by bidding me walk these streets, like St Denis, with my head in my hand. I have no other proof. I can call no other witness. He can deliver me if He will."

There was a sudden silence, which was somehow stronger than a pause; and in it Armitage could be heard saying sharply, and almost querulously: "Why, here's Gale again, after all. Have you dropped from the sky?"

Gale was indeed sauntering in a clear space round the corner of the statue with all the appearance of having just arrived at a crowded At Home; and Bertrand was quick to seize the chance of an anticlimax to the hermit's oratory.

"This," he cried, "is a gentleman who thinks he can find the body himself. Have you brought it with you, monsieur?"

The joke about the poet as detective had already been passed round among many people, and the suggestion received a new kind of applause. Somebody called out in a high, piping voice, "He's got it in his pocket"; and another, in deep sepulchral tones, "His waistcoat pocket."

Mr Gale certainly had his hands in his pockets, whether or no he had anything else in them; and it was with great nonchalance that he replied: "Well, in that sense, I suppose I haven't got it. But you have."

The next moment he had astonished his friends, who were not used to seeing him so alert, by leaping on the chair, and himself addressing the crowd in clear tones, and in excellent French: "Well, my friends," he said, "the first thing I have to do is to associate myself with everything said by my honourable friend, if he will allow me to call him so, about the merits and high moral qualities of the late Professor Boyg. Boyg, at any rate, is in every way worthy of all the honour you can pay to him. Whatever else is doubtful, whatever else we differ about, we can all salute in him that search for truth which is the most disinterested of all our duties to God. I agree with my friend Dr Garth that he deserves to have a statue, not only in his own town, but in every town in the world."

The anti-clericals began to cheer warmly, while their opponents watched in silence, wondering where this last eccentric development might lead. The poet seemed to realize their mystification, and smiled as he continued: "Perhaps you wonder why I should say that so emphatically. Well, I suppose you all have your own reasons for recognizing this genuine love of truth in the late Professor. But I say it because I happen to know something that perhaps you don't know, which makes me specially certain about his honesty."

"And what is that?" asked Father Bernard, in the pause that followed.

"Because," said Gale, "he was going to see Father Hyacinth to own himself wrong."

Bertrand made a swift movement forward that seemed almost to threaten an assault: but Garth arrested it, and Gale went on, without noticing it.

"Professor Boyg had discovered that his theory was wrong after all. That was the sensational discovery he had made in those last days and with those last experiments. I suspected it when I compared the current tale with his reputation as a simple and kindly man. I did not believe he would have gone merely to triumph over his worst enemy; it was far more probable that he thought it a point of honour to acknowledge his mistake. For, without professing to know much about these things, I am sure it was a mistake. Things do not, after all, need all those thousand years to petrify in that particular fashion. Under certain conditions, which chemists could explain better than I, they do not need more than one year, or even one day. Something in the properties of the local water, applied or intensified by special methods, can really in a few hours turn an animal organism into a fossil. The scientific experiment has been made; and the proof is before you."

He made a gesture with his hand, and went on, with something more like excitement:

"M. Bertrand is right in saying that truth is not in a well, but on a tower. It is on a pedestal. You have looked at it every day. There is the body of Boyg!"

And he pointed to the statue in the middle of the market-place, wreathed with laurel and defaced with stones, as it had stood so long in that quiet square, and looked down at so many casual passers-by.

"Somebody suggested just now," he went on, glancing over a sea of gaping faces, "that I carried the statue in my waistcoat pocket. Well, I don't carry all of it, of course, but this is a part of it," and he took out a small object like a stick of grey chalk; "this is a finger of it knocked off by a stone. I picked it up by the pedestal. If anybody who understands these things likes to look at it, he will agree that the consistency is precisely the same as the admitted fossils in the geological museum."

He held it out to them, but the whole mob stood still as if it also was a mob of men turned to stone.

"Perhaps you think I'm mad," he said pleasantly. "Well, I'm not exactly mad, but I have an odd sort of sympathy with madmen. I can manage them better than most people can, because I can fancy somehow the wild way their minds will work. I understand the man who did this. I know he did, because I talked to him for half the morning; and it's exactly the sort of thing he would do. And when first I heard talk of fossil shells and petrified insects and so on, I did the same thing that such men always do. I exaggerated it into a sort of extravagant vision, a vision of fossil forests, and fossil cattle, and fossil elephants and camels; and so, naturally, to another thought: a coincidence that somehow turned me cold. A Fossil Man.

"It was then that I looked up at the statue; and knew it was not a statue. It was a corpse petrified by the curious chemistry of your strange mountain stream. I call it a fossil as a loose popular term; of course I know enough geology to know it is not the correct term. But I was not exactly concerned with a problem of geology. I was concerned with what some prefer to call criminology and I prefer to call crime. If that extraordinary erection was the corpse, who and where was the criminal? Who was the assassin who had set up the dead man to be at once obvious and invisible; and had, so to speak, hidden him in the broad daylight? Well, you have all heard the arguments about the stream and the scrap of paper, and up to a point I have entirely followed them. Everyone agreed that the secret was somewhere hidden on that bare hill where there was nothing but the glass-roofed studio and the lonely hermitage; and suspicion centred entirely upon the hermitage. For the man in the studio was a fervent friend of the man who was murdered, and one of those rejoicing most heartily at what he had discovered. But perhaps you have rather forgotten what he really had discovered. His real discovery was of the sort that infuriates friends and not foes. The man who has the courage to say he is wrong has to face the worst hatred; the hatred of those who think he is right. Boyg's final discovery, like our final discovery, rather reverses the relations of those two little houses on the hill. Even if Father Hyacinth had been a fiend instead of a saint, he had no possible motive to prevent his enemy from offering him a public apology. It was a believer in Boygism who struck down Boyg. It was his follower who became his pursuer and persecutor; who at least turned in unreasonable fury upon him. It was Paradou the sculptor who snatched up a chisel and struck his philosophical teacher, at the end of some furious argument about the theory which the artist had valued only as a wild inspiration, being quite indifferent to the tame question of its truth. I don't think he meant to kill Boyg; I doubt whether anybody could possibly prove he did; and even if he did, I rather doubt whether he can be held responsible for that or for anything else. But though Paradou may be a lunatic, he is also a logician; and there is one more interesting logical step in this story.

"I met Paradou myself this morning; owing to my good luck in putting my leg through his skylight. He also has his theories and controversies; and this morning he was very controversial. As I say, I had a long argument with him, all about realism in sculpture. I know many people will tell you that nothing has ever come out of arguments; and I tell you that everything has always come out of arguments; and anyhow, if you want to know what has come out of this, you've got to understand this argument. Everybody was always jeering at poor old Paradou as a sculptor and saying he turned men into monsters; that his figures had flat heads like snakes, or sagging knees like elephants, or humps like human camels. And he was always shouting back at them, 'Yes, and eyes like blindworms when it comes to seeing your own hideous selves! This is what you *do* look like, you ugly brutes! These are the crooked, clownish, lumpish attitudes in which you really do stand; only a lot of lying fashionable portrait painters have persuaded you that you look like Graces and Greek gods.' He was at it hammer and tongs with me this morning; and I dare say I was lucky he didn't finish that argument with a chisel. But anyhow the argument wasn't started then. It all came upon him with a rush, when he had committed his real though probably unintentional killing. As he stood staring at the corpse, there arose out of the very abyss of his disappointment the vision of a strange vengeance or reparation. He began to see the vast outlines of a joke as gigantic as the Great Pyramid. He would set up that grim granite jest in the market-place, to grin for ever at his critics and detractors. The dead man himself had just been explaining to him the process by which the water of that place would rapidly petrify organic substances. The notes and documents of his proof lay scattered about the studio where he had fallen. His own proof should be applied to his own body, for a purpose of which he had never dreamed. If the sculptor simply lifted the body in the ungainly attitude in which it had actually fallen, if he froze or fixed it in the stream, or set it upon the public pedestal, it would be the very thing about which he had so bitterly debated; a real man, in a real posture, held up to the scorn of men.

"That insane genius promised himself a lonely laughter, and a secret superiority to all his enemies, in hearing the critics discuss it as the crazy creation of a crank sculptor. He looked forward to the groups that would stand before the statue, and prove the anatomy to be wrong, and clearly demonstrate the posture to be impossible. And he would listen, and laugh inwardly like a true lunatic, knowing that they were proving the utter unreality of a real man. That being his dream, he had no difficulty in carrying it out. He had no need to hide the body; he had it brought down from his studio, not secretly but publicly and even pompously, the finished work of a great sculptor escorted by the devotees of a great discoverer. But indeed, Boyg was something more than a man who made a discovery; and there is, in comparison, a sort of cant even in the talk of a man having the courage to discover it. What other man would have had the courage to undiscover it? That monument that hides a strange sin, hides a much stranger and much rarer virtue. Yes, you do well to hail it as a true scientific trophy. That is the statue of Boyg the Undiscoverer. That cold chimera of the rock is not only the abortion born of some horrible chemical change; it is the outcome of a nobler experiment, which attests for ever the honour and probity of science. You may well praise him as a man of science; for he, at least, in an affair of science, acted like a man. You may well set up statues to him as a hero of science; for he was more of a hero in being wrong than he could ever have been in being right. And though the stars have seen rise, from the soils and substance of our native star, no such monstrosity as that man of stone, heaven may look down with more wonder at the man than at the monster. And we of all schools and of all philosophies can pass it like a funeral procession taking leave of an illustrious grave and, like soldiers, salute it as we pass."

VI

The House of the Peacock

It happened that some years ago, down a sunny and empty street of suburban gardens and villas, a young man was walking; a young man in rather outlandish clothes and almost prehistoric hat; for he was newly come to London from a very remote and sleepy small town in the West Country. There was nothing else especially remarkable about him, except what happened to him; which was certainly remarkable, not to say regrettable. There cannonaded into him an elderly gentleman running down the street, breathless, bare-headed, and in festive evening dress, who immediately caught him by the lapels of his antiquated coat and asked him to dinner. It would be truer to say that he implored him to come to dinner. As the bewildered provincial did not know him, or anybody else for miles round, the situation seemed singular; but the provincial, vaguely supposing it to be a hospitable ceremony peculiar to London town, where the streets were paved with gold, finally consented. He went to the hospitable mansion, which was only a few doors down the road; and he was never seen again in the land of the living.

None of the ordinary explanations would seem to have fitted the case. The men were total strangers. The man from the country carried no papers or valuables or money worth mentioning; and certainly did not look in the least as if he were likely to carry them. And, on the other hand, his host had the outward marks of almost offensive prosperity; a gleam of satin in the linings of his clothes, a glitter of opalescent stones in his studs and cuff-links, a cigar that seemed to perfume the street. The guest could hardly have been decoyed with the ordinary motive of robbery, or of any form of fraud. And indeed the motive with which he really was decoyed was one of the queerest in the world; so queer that a man might have a hundred guesses before he hit on it.

It is doubtful whether anyone ever would have hit on it, but for the extra touch of eccentricity which happened to distinguish another young man, who happened to be walking down the same street an hour or two afterwards on the same sunny afternoon. It must not be supposed that he brought to the problem any of the dexterities of a detective; least of all of the usual detective of romance, who solves problems by the closest attention to everything and the promptest presence of mind. It would be truer to say of this man that he sometimes solved them by absence of mind. Some solitary object he was staring at would become fixed in his mind like a talisman, and he stared at it till it began to speak to him like an oracle. On other occasions a stone, a starfish, or a canary had thus riveted his eye and seemed to reply to his questions. On the present occasion his text was less trivial from an ordinary standpoint; but it was some time before his own standpoint could be ordinary. He had drifted along the sunny suburban road, drinking in a certain drowsy pleasure in seeing where the laburnum made lines of gold in the green, or patches of white or red thorn glowed in the growing shadows; for the sunshine was taking on the tinge of sunset. But for the most part he was contented to see the green semicircles of lawn repeat themselves like a pattern of green moons; for he was not one to whom repetition was merely monotony. Only in looking over a particular gate at a particular lawn, he became pleasantly conscious, or half-conscious, of a new note of colour in the greenness; a much bluer green, which seemed to change to vivid blue, as the object at which he was gazing moved sharply, turning a small head on a long neck. It was a peacock. But he had thought of a thousand things before he thought of the obvious thing. The burning blue of the plumage on the neck had reminded him of blue fire, and blue fire had reminded him of some dark fantasy about blue devils, before he had fully realized even that it was a peacock he was staring at. And the tail, that trailing tapestry of eyes, had led his wandering wits away to those dark but divine monsters of the Apocalypse whose eyes were multiplied like their wings, before he had remembered that a peacock, even in a more practical sense, was an odd thing to see in so ordinary a setting.

For Gabriel Gale, as the young man was called, was a minor poet, but something of a major painter; and, in his capacity of celebrity and lover of landscape, he had been invited often enough into those larger landscape gardens of the landed aristocracy, where peacocks as pets are not uncommon. The very thought of such country seats brought back to him the memory of one of them, decayed and neglected indeed compared with most, but having for him the almost unbearable beauty of a lost paradise. He saw standing for a moment in such glimmering grass a figure statelier than any peacock, the colours of whose dress burned blue with a vivid sadness that might indeed be symbolized by a blue devil. But when intellectual fancies and emotional regrets had alike rolled away, there remained a more rational perplexity. After all, a peacock was an unusual thing to see in the front garden of a small suburban villa. It seemed somehow too big for the place, as if it would knock down the little trees when it spread its tail. It was like visiting a maiden lady in lodgings, who might be expected to keep a bird, and finding that she kept an ostrich.

These more practical reflections in their turn had passed through his mind before he came to the most practical reflection of all – that for the last five minutes he had been leaning on somebody else's front gate with all the air of repose and finality of a rustic leaning on his own stile. Comment might have been aroused if anybody had come out; but nobody came out. On the contrary, somebody went in. As the peacock again turned its tiny crown and trailed away towards the house, the poet calmly opened the garden gate and stepped across the grass, following in the track of the bird. The darkening twilight of that garden was enriched by masses of red may, and altogether the villa had the look of being cruder and more cockney than the grounds in which it stood. Indeed, it was either actually unfinished or undergoing some new alterations and repairs, for a ladder leaned against the wall apparently to allow workmen to reach an upper storey; and, moreover, there were marks of bushes having been cut or cleared away, perhaps for some new plan of building. Red bunches thus gathered from the bushes were stacked on the window-sill of the upper storey, and a few petals seemed to have dropped on the ladder, indicating that they had been carried up by that route. All these things the gaze of Gale gradually took in, as he stood with a rather bewildered air at the foot of the ladder. He felt the contrast between the unfinished house with the ladder and the rich garden with the peacock. It was almost as if the aristocratic birds and bushes had been there before the bourgeois bricks and mortar.

He had a curious innocence which often appeared as impudence. Like other human beings, he was quite capable of doing wrong knowingly and being ashamed of it. But so long as he meant no wrong, it never even occurred to him that there could be anything to be ashamed of. For him burglary meant stealing; and he might have strolled, so to speak, down the chimney into a king's bedchamber, so long as he had no intent to steal. The invitation of the leaning ladder and the open window was something almost too obvious even to be called an adventure. He began to mount the ladder as if he were going up the front steps of an hotel. But when he came to the upper rungs he seemed to stop a moment, frowned at something; and, accelerating his ascent, slipped quickly over the window-sill into the room.

The twilight of the room seemed like darkness after the golden glare of the evening sunlight, and it was a second or two before the glimmer of light reflected from a round mirror opposite enabled him to make out the main features of the interior. The room itself seemed dusty and even defaced; the dark blue–green hangings, of a peacock pattern, as if carrying out the same scheme as the living decoration of the garden, were themselves, nevertheless, a background of dead colours; and, peering into the dusty mirror, he saw it was cracked. Nevertheless, the neglected room was evidently partly redecorated for a new festivity, for a long table was elaborately laid out for a dinner-party. By every plate was a group of quaint and varied glasses for the wines of every course; and the blue vases on the table and the mantelpiece were filled with the same red and white blooms from the garden which he had seen on the window-sill. Nevertheless, there were odd things about the dinner-table, and his first thought was that it had already been the scene of some struggle or stampede, in which the salt-cellar had been knocked over and, for all he knew, the looking-glass broken. Then he looked at the knives on the table, and a light was beginning to dawn in his eyes, when the door opened and a sturdy, grey-haired man came rapidly into the room.

And at that he came back to common sense like a man flung from a flying ship into the cold shock of the sea. He remembered suddenly where he was and how he had got there. It was characteristic of him that, though he saw a practical point belatedly – and, perhaps, too late – when he did see it he saw it lucidly in all its logical ramifications. Nobody would believe in any legitimate reason for entering a strange house by the window instead of knocking at the door. Also, as it happened, he had no legitimate reason – or none that he could explain without a lecture on poetry and philosophy. He even realized the ugly detail that he was at that very moment fidgeting with the knives on the table, and that a large number of them were silver. After an instant of hesitation, he put down the knife and politely removed his hat.

"Well," he said at last, with inconsequent irony, "I shouldn't shoot if I were you; but I suppose you'll send for the police."

The newcomer, who was apparently the householder, was also fixed for the moment in a somewhat baffling attitude. When first he opened the door he had given a convulsive start, had opened his mouth as if to shout, and shut it again grimly, as if he was not even going to speak. He was a man with a strong, shrewd face, spoilt by painfully prominent eyes which gave him a look of perpetual protest. But by some accident it was not at these accusing eyes that the sleepy blue eyes of the poetical burglar were directed. The trick by which his rambling eye was so often riveted by some trivial object led him to look no higher at the moment than the stud in the old gentleman's shirt-front, which was an unusually large and luminous opal. Having uttered his highly perverse and even suicidal remark, the poet smiled as if in relief, and waited for the other to speak.

"Are you a burglar?" asked the owner of the house at last.

"To make a clean breast of it, I'm not," answered Gale. "But if you ask me what else I am, I really don't know."

The other man came rapidly round the table towards him, and made a motion as if offering his hand, or even both his hands.

"Of course you're a burglar," he said; "but it doesn't matter. Won't you stay to dinner?"

Then, after a sort of agitated pause, he repeated: "Come, you really must stay to dinner; there's a place laid for you."

Gale looked gravely along the table and counted the number of places laid for dinner. The number disposed of any final doubts he might have had about the meaning of this string of eccentricities. He knew why the host wore opals, and why the mirror had been deliberately broken and why the salt was spilt, and why the knives shone on the table in a pattern of crosses, and why the eccentric householder brought may into the house, and why he decorated it with peacocks' feathers, and even had a peacock in the garden. He realized that the ladder did not stand where it did to permit people to climb by it to the window, but merely that they might pass under it on entering the door. And he realized that he was the thirteenth man to sit down at that banquet.

"Dinner is just coming in," said the man with the opals with eager amiability. "I'm just going down to fetch the other fellows up. You'll find them very interesting company, I assure you; no nonsense about them; shrewd, sharp fellows out against all this superstitious nonsense. My name is Crundle, Humphrey Crundle, and I'm pretty well known in the business world. I suppose I must introduce myself in order to introduce you to the others."

Gale was vaguely conscious that his absent-minded eye had often rested on the name of Crundle, associated with some soap or lozenge or fountain-pen; and, little as he knew of such things, he could imagine that such an advertiser, though he lived in a little villa, could afford peacocks and five different kinds of wine. But other thoughts were already oppressing his imagination, and he looked in a somewhat sombre fashion out on to the garden of the peacock, where the sunset light was dying on the lawn.

The members of the Thirteen Club, as they came trooping up the stairs and settled into their seats, seemed for the most part to be at least quite ready for their dinner. Most of them had a rather rollicking attitude, which in some took the more vivid form of vulgarity. A few who were quite young, clerks and possibly dependents, had foolish and nervous faces, as if they were doing something a little too daring. Two of them stood out from the company by the singularity of being obviously gentlemen. One of these was a little dried-up old gentleman, with a face that was a labyrinth of wrinkles, on the top of which was perched a very obvious chestnut wig. He was introduced as Sir Daniel Creed, and was apparently a barrister of note in his day, though the day seemed a little distant. The other, who was merely presented as Mr Noel, was more interesting: a tall, stalwart man of dubious age but indubitable intelligence, even in the first glance of his eyes. His features were handsome in a large and craggy fashion; but the hollows of the temples and the sunken framework of the eyes gave him a look of fatigue that was mental and not physical. The poet's impalpable intuitions told him that the appearance was not misleading – that the man who had thus come into this odd Society had been in many odd societies, probably seeking for something more odd than he had ever found.

It was some time, however, before any of these guests could show anything of their quality, owing to the abounding liveliness and loquacity of their host. Mr Crundle may, perhaps, have thought it appropriate in a President of a Thirteen Club to talk thirteen to the dozen. Anyhow, for some time he talked for the whole company, rolling about in his chair in radiant satisfaction, like a man who has at last realized his wildest vision of happiness. Indeed, there was something almost abnormal about the gaiety and vivacity of this grey-haired merchant; it seemed to be fed from a fountain within him that owed nothing to the circumstances of festivity. The remarks with which he pelted everybody were often rather random, but always uproariously entertaining to himself. Gale could only dimly speculate on what he would be like when he had emptied all the five glasses in front of him. But, indeed, he was destined to show himself in more than one strange aspect before those glasses were emptied.

It was after one of his repeated assertions that these stories about bad luck were all the same sort of damned nonsense that the keen though quavering voice of old Creed got a word in edgeways.

"There, my dear Crundle, I would make a distinction," he said in a legal manner. "They are all damned nonsense, but they are not all the same sort of damned nonsense. As a point of historical research, they seem to me to differ in rather a singular fashion. The origin of some is obvious, of others highly obscure. The fancies about Friday and thirteen have probably a religious basis; but what, for instance, can be the basis of objecting to peacocks' feathers?"

Crundle was replying with a joyful roar that it was some infernal rubbish or other, when Gale, who had quickly slipped into a seat beside the man called Noel, interposed in a conversational manner.

"I fancy I can throw a little light on that. I believe I found a trace of it in looking at some old illuminated manuscripts of the ninth or tenth century. There is a very curious design, in a stiff Byzantine style, representing the two armies preparing for the war in heaven. But St. Michael is handing out spears to the good angels; while Satan is elaborately arming the rebel angels with peacocks' feathers."

Noel turned his hollow eyes sharply in the direction of the speaker. "That is really interesting," he said; "you mean it was all that old theological notion of the wickedness of pride?"

"Well, there's a whole peacock in the garden for you to pluck," cried Crundle in his boisterous manner, "if any of you want to go out fighting angels."

"They are not very effective weapons," said Gale gravely, "and I fancy that is what the artist in the Dark Ages must have meant. There seems to me to be something that rather hits the wrong imperialism in the right place, about the contrast in the weapon; the fact that the right side was arming for a real and therefore doubtful battle, while the wrong side was already, so to speak, handing out the palms of victory. You cannot fight anybody with the palms of victory."

Crundle showed a curious restlessness as this conversation proceeded; and a much less radiant restlessness than before.

His prominent eyes shot questions at the speakers, his mouth worked, and his fingers began to drum on the table. At last he broke out:

"What's all this mean, eh? One would think you were half on the side of all the stuff and nonsense – all of you talking about it with those long faces."

"Pardon me," interposed the old lawyer, with a relish for repeating the logical point, "my suggestion was very simple. I spoke of causes, not of justifications. I say the cause of the peacock legend is less apparent than that of the bad luck of Friday."

"Do you think Friday unlucky?" demanded Crundle, like one at bay, turning his starting eyes on the poet.

"No, I think Friday lucky," answered Gale. "All Christian people, whatever their lighter superstitions, have always thought Friday lucky. Otherwise they would have talked about Bad Friday instead of Good Friday."

"Oh, Christians be – " began Mr Crundle with sudden violence; but he was stopped by something in the voice of Noel that seemed to make his violence a vain splutter.

"I'm not a Christian," said Noel in a voice like stone. "It is useless now to wonder whether I wish I were. But it seems to me that Mr Gale's point is a perfectly fair one; that such a religion might well actually contradict such a superstition. And it seems to me also that the truth might be applied yet further. If I believed in God, I should not believe in a God who made happiness depend on knocking over a salt-cellar or seeing a peacock's feather. Whatever Christianity teaches, I presume it does not teach that the Creator is crazy."

Gale nodded thoughtfully, as if in partial assent, and answered rather as if he were addressing Noel alone, in the middle of a wilderness.

"In that sense of course you are right," he said. "But I think there is a little more to be said on the matter. I think most people, as I say, have really taken these superstitions rather lightly, perhaps more lightly than you do. And I think they mostly referred to lighter evils, in that world of rough-and-tumble circumstance which they thought of rather as connected with elves than with angels. But, after all, Christians admit more than one kind even of angels; and some of them are fallen angels – like the people with the peacocks' feathers. Now I have a feeling that *they* might really have to do with peacocks' feathers. Just as lower spirits play low tricks with tables and tambourines, they might play low tricks with knives and salt-cellars. Certainly our souls do not depend on a broken mirror; but there's nothing an unclean spirit would like better than to make us think so. Whether he succeeds depends on the spirit in which we break it. And I can imagine that breaking the mirror in a certain moral spirit – as, for instance, a spirit of scorn and inhumanity – might bring one in touch with lower influences. I can imagine that a cloud might rest on the house where such a thing was done, and evil spirits cluster about it."

There was a rather singular silence, a silence that seemed to the speaker to brood and settle even upon the gardens and streets beyond; no one spoke; the silence was punctuated at last by the thin and piercing cry of a peacock.

Then it was that Humphrey Crundle startled them all with his first outbreak. He had been staring at the speaker with bursting eyeballs; at length, when he found his voice, it was so thick and hoarse that the first note of it was hardly more human than the bird's. He stuttered and stammered with rage, and it was only towards the end of the first sentence that he was even intelligible. "...Coming here and jabbering blasted drivel and drinking my burgundy like a lord; talking rubbish against our whole...against the very first...why don't you pull our noses as well? Why the hell don't you pull our noses?"

"Come, come," cut in Noel in his trenchant tones, "you are getting unreasonable, Crundle; I understand that this gentleman came here at your own invitation, to take the place of one of our friends."

"I understood Arthur Bailey sent a wire that he was detained," observed the more precise lawyer, "and that Mr Gale had kindly taken his place."

"Yes," snapped Crundle, "I asked him to sit down as thirteenth man, and that alone smashes your superstition; for considering how he came in, he's jolly lucky to get a good dinner."

Noel again interposed with a remonstrance; but Gale had already risen to his feet. He did not seem annoyed, but rather distrait; and he addressed himself to Creed and Noel, neglecting his excitable host.

"I am much obliged to you gentlemen," he said, "but I think I shall be going. It is quite true that I was invited to the dinner, but hardly to the house – well, I can't help having a curious notion about it."

He played for a moment with the crossed knives on the table; then he said, looking out into the garden –

"The truth is I'm not sure the thirteenth man has been so lucky after all."

"What do you mean?" cried his host sharply. "Dare you say you haven't had a good dinner? You're not going to pretend you've been poisoned."

Gale was still looking out of the window; and he said without moving: "I am the fourteenth man, and I did not pass under the ladder."

It was characteristic of old Creed that he could only follow the logical argument in a literal fashion, and missed the symbol and the spiritual atmosphere which the subtler Noel had already understood. For the first time the old lawyer in the red wig really looked a little senile. He blinked at Gale and said querulously: "You don't mean to say you'd bother to keep all those rules about ladders and things?"

"I'm not sure I should bother to keep them," replied Gale, "but I am sure I shouldn't bother to break them. One seems to break so many other things when one begins to break them.

126

There are many things that are almost as easy to break as a looking-glass." He paused a moment, and added as if in apology: "There are the Ten Commandments, you know."

There was another abrupt accidental silence, and Noel found himself listening with irrational rigidity for the ugly voice of the beautiful bird outside. But it did not speak. He had the subconscious and still more meaningless fancy that it had been strangled in the dark.

Then the poet for the first time turned his face to Humphrey Crundle, and looked straight into the goggling eyes as he spoke.

"Peacocks may not be unlucky; but pride is unlucky. And it was in insolence and contempt that you set yourself to trample on the traditions or the follies of humbler men; so that you have come to trample on a holier thing at last. Cracked mirrors may not be unlucky; but cracked brains are unlucky; and you have gone mad on reason and common sense till you are a criminal lunatic this day. And red may need not be unlucky; but there is something that is more red and much more unlucky; and there are spots of it on the window-sill and on the steps of the ladder. I took it for the red petals myself."

For the first time in his restless hour of hospitality the man at the head of the table sat perfectly still. Something in his sudden and stony immobility seemed to startle all the rest into life, and they all sprang to their feet with a confused clamour of protest and question. Noel alone seemed to keep his head under the shock.

"Mr Gale," he said firmly, "you have said too much or too little. A good many people would say you were talking a lot of lurid nonsense, but I have a notion that what you talk is not always such nonsense as it sounds. But if you leave it as it is, it will be simply unsupported slander. In plain words, you say there has been a crime here. Whom do you accuse; or are we all to accuse each other?"

"I do not accuse you," answered Gale, "and the proof is that if it must be verified, you had better verify it yourself. Sir Daniel Creed is a lawyer, and may very properly accompany you. Go and look yourselves at the marks on the ladder. You will find some more in the grass round the foot of the ladder, leading away in the direction of that big dustbin in the corner of the garden. I think it would be as well if you looked in the dustbin. It may be the end of your search."

Old Crundle continued to sit like a graven image; and something told them that his goggle eyes were now, as it were, turned inward. He was revolving some enigma of his own which seemed to baffle and blind him, so that the whole disordered scene broke about him unnoticed. Creed and Noel left the room and could be heard running down the stairs, and talking in low voices under the window. Then their voices died away in the direction of the dustbin; and still the old man sat with the opal on his breast, as still as an Eastern idol with its sacred gem. Then he seemed suddenly to dilate and glow as if a monstrous lamp had been lit within him. He sprang to his feet, brandished his goblet as if for a toast, and brought it down again on the table so that the glass was shattered and the wine spilt in a blood-red star.

"I've got it; I was right," he cried in a sort of exaltation. "I was right; I was right after all. Don't you see, all of you? Don't you see? That man out there isn't the thirteenth man. He's really the fourteenth man, and the fellow here is the fifteenth. Arthur Bailey's the real thirteenth man, and he's all right, isn't he? He didn't actually come to the house, but why should that matter? Why the devil should that matter? He's the thirteenth member of the club, isn't he? There can't be any more thirteenth men afterwards, can there? I don't care a curse about all the rest; I don't care what you call me or what you do to me. I say all this fool's poetical stuff goes to pot, because the man in the dustbin isn't number thirteen at all, and I challenge anybody – "

Noel and Creed were standing in the room with very grim faces as the man at the head of the table gabbled on with a frightful volubility. When he gasped and choked for a moment with the rush of his own words, Noel said in a voice of steel:

"I am sorry to say that you were right."

"Most horrible thing I ever saw in my life," said old Creed, and sat down suddenly, lifting a liqueur glass of cognac with a shaking hand.

"The body of an unfortunate man with his throat cut had been concealed in the dustbin," went on Noel in a lifeless voice. "By the mark on his clothes, which are curiously old-fashioned for a comparatively young man, he seems to have come from Stoke-under-Ham."

"What was he like?" asked Gale with sudden animation.

Noel looked at him curiously. "He was very long and lank, with hair like tow," he replied. "What do you mean?"

"I guessed he must have looked a little like me," answered the poet.

Crundle had collapsed in his chair again after his last and strangest outbreak, and made no attempt at explanation or escape. His mouth was still moving, but he was talking to himself; proving with ever-increasing lucidity and repetition that the man he had murdered had no right to the number thirteen. Sir Daniel Creed seemed for the moment almost as stricken and silent a figure; but it was he who broke the silence. Lifting his bowed head with its grotesque wig, he said suddenly: "This blood cries for justice. I am an old man, but I would avenge it on my own brother."

"I am just going to telephone for the police," said Noel quietly. "I can see no cause for hesitation." His large figure and features looked notably less languid, and his hollow eyes had a glow in them.

A big florid man named Bull, of the commercial traveller type, who had been very noisy and convivial at the other end of the table, now began to take the stage like the foreman of a jury. It was rather typical of him that he waited for more educated people to lead, and then proceeded to lead them.

"No cause for hesitation. No case for sentimentalism," he trumpeted as healthily as an elephant. "Painful business, of course; old member of the club and all that. But I say I'm no sentimentalist; and whoever did this deserves hanging. Well, there's no doubt of who did it. We heard him practically confess a minute ago, when these gentlemen were out of the room."

"Always thought he was a bad lot," said one of the clerks; possibly a clerk with an old score of his own.

"I am all for acting at once," said Noel. "Where is the telephone?"

Gabriel Gale stepped in front of the collapsed figure in the chair, and turned his face to the advancing crowd.

"Stop," he cried, "let me say a word."

"Well, what is it?" asked Noel steadily.

"I do not like boasting," said the poet, "but unfortunately the argument can only take that form. I am a sentimentalist, as Mr Bull would say; I am by trade a sentimentalist; a mere scribbler of sentimental songs. You are all very hard-headed, rational, sensible people who laugh at superstitions; you are practical men, and men of commonsense. But your commonsense didn't discover the dead body. You would have smoked your practical cigars and drunk your practical grog and gone home all over smiles, leaving it to rot in the dustbin. *You* never found out where your rational sceptical road can lead a man, as it has led that poor gibbering idiot in the chair. A sentimentalist, a dabbler in moonshine, found out that for you; perhaps because he was a sentimentalist. For I really have a streak in me of the moonshine that leads such men astray; that is why I can follow them. And now the lucky sentimentalist must say a word for the unlucky one."

"Do you mean for the criminal?" asked Creed in his sharp but shaky voice.

"Yes," replied Gale. "I discovered him and I defend him."

"So you defend murderers, do you?" demanded Bull.

"Some murderers," answered Gale calmly. "This one was a rather unique sort of murderer. In fact, I am far from certain that he was a murderer at all. It may have been an accident. It may have been a sort of mechanical action, almost like an automaton."

The light of long-lost cross-examinations gleamed in Creed's aged eyes, and his sharp voice no longer shook.

"You mean to say," he said, "that Crundle read a telegram from Bailey, realized there was a vacant place, went out into the street and talked to a total stranger, brought him in here, went somewhere to fetch a razor or a carving-knife, cut his guest's throat, carried the corpse down the ladder, and carefully covered it with the lid of the dustbin. And he did all that by accident, or by an automatic gesture."

"Very well put, Sir Daniel," answered Gale; "and now let me put you a question, in the same logical style. In your legal language, what about motive? You say he could not assassinate a total stranger by accident; but why should he assassinate a total stranger on purpose? On what purpose? It not only served no end he had in view; it actually ruined everything he had in view. Why in the world should he want to make a gap in his Thirteen Club dinner? Why in the name of wonder should *he* want to make the thirteenth man a monument of disaster? His own crime was at the expense of his own creed, or cranky doubt, denial, or whatever you call it."

"That is true," assented Noel, "and what is the meaning of it all?"

"I do believe," replied Gale, "that nobody can tell you but myself; and I will tell you why. Do you realize how full life is of awkward attitudes? You get them in snapshots; I suppose the new ugly schools of art are trying to snap them; figures leaning stiffly, standing on one leg, resting unconscious hands on incongruous objects. This is a tragedy of awkward positions. I can understand it because I myself, this very afternoon, was in the devil of an awkward position.

"I had climbed in through that window simply out of silly curiosity, and I was standing at the table like a fool, picking up the knives and putting them straight. I still had my hat on, but when Crundle came in I made a movement to take it off with the knife still in my hand; then I corrected myself and put the knife down first. You know those tiny confused movements one sometimes has. Now Crundle, when he first saw me, and before he saw me close, staggered as if I had been God Almighty or the hangman waiting in his dining-room; and I think I know why. I am awkward and tall and tow-haired, too; and I was standing there dark against the daylight where the other had stood. It must have seemed as if the corpse had lifted the dustbin lid and crawled back up the ladder, and taken up his station like a ghost. But meanwhile my own little irresolute gesture with the half-lifted knife had told me something. It had told me what really happened.

"When that poor rustic from Somerset strayed into this room he was what perhaps none of us can be, he was shocked. He came of some old rural type that really did believe in such omens. He hastily picked up one of the crossed knives and was putting it straight when he caught sight of the heap of spilt salt. Possibly he thought his own gesture had spilt it. At that crucial instant Crundle entered the room, adding to the confusion of his guest and hastening his hurried attempt at doing two things at once. The unhappy guest, with fingers still clutched round the knife-handle, made a grab at the salt and tried to toss some of it over his shoulder. In the same flash the fanatic in the doorway had leapt upon him like a panther and was tugging at the lifted wrist.

"For all Crundle's crazy universe was rocking in that instant. You, who talk of superstitions, have you realized that this house is a house of spells? Don't you know it is chock full of charms and magic rites, only they are all done backwards, as the witches said the Lord's Prayer? Can you imagine how a witch would feel if two words of the prayer came right by accident? Crundle saw that this clown from the country was reversing all the spells of his own black art. If salt was once thrown over the shoulder, all the great work might yet be undone. With all the strength he could call from hell he hung on to the hand with the knife, caring only to prevent a few grains of silver dust from drifting to the floor.

"God alone knows if it was an accident. I do not say it as an idle phrase. That single split second, and all that was really hidden in it, lies open before God as large and luminous as an eternity. But I am a man and he is a man; and I will not give a man to the gallows, if I can help it, for what may have been accidental or automatic or even a sort of self-defence. But if any of you will take a knife and a pinch of salt and put yourself in the poor fellow's position, you will see exactly what happened. All I say is this; that at no time and in no way, perhaps, could things have been precisely in that posture, and the edge of a knife been so near to a man's throat without intention on either side, except by this one particular tangle of trivialities that has led up to this one particular tragedy. It is strange to think of that poor yokel setting out from his far-off Somerset village, with his little handful of local legends, and this brooding eccentric and scoffer rushing out of this villa full of rage of his hobby, and their ending locked in this one unique and ungainly grapple, a wrestle between two superstitions."

The figure at the head of the table had been almost forgotten like a piece of furniture; but Noel turned his eyes slowly towards it, and said with a cold patience as if to an exasperating child: "Is all this true?"

Crundle sprang unsteadily to his feet, his mouth still working, and they saw at the edge of it a touch of foam.

"What I want to know," he began in a resonant voice; and then the voice seemed to dry up in his throat and he swayed twice and pitched forward on the table amid the wreck of his own wine and crystal.

"I don't know about a policeman," said Noel; "but we shall have to send for a doctor."

"You will want two doctors for what will have to be done to him," said Gale; and walked towards the window by which he had come in.

Noel walked with him to the garden gate, past the peacock and the green lawn, that looked almost as blue as the peacock under a strong moonlight. When the poet was outside the gate, he turned and said a last word.

"You are Norman Noel, the great traveller, I think. You interest me more than that unfortunate monomaniac did; and I want to ask you a question. Forgive me if I imagine things for you, so to speak; it is a way I have. You have studied superstitions all over the world, and you have seen things compared with which all that talk of salt and table knives is like a child's game of consequences. You have been in the dark forests over which the vampire seems to pass more vast than a dragon; or in the mountains of the werewolf, where men say a man can see in the face of his friend or his wife the eyes of a wild beast. You have known people who had real superstitions; black, towering, terrific superstitions; you have lived with those people; and I want to ask you a question about them."

"You seem to know something about them yourself," answered Noel; "but I will answer any question you like."

"Were they not happier men than you?"

Gale paused a moment as he put the question, and then went on. "Did they not in fact sing more songs, and dance more dances, and drink wine with more real merriment? That was because they believed in evil. In evil spells, perhaps, in evil luck, in evil under all sorts of stupid and ignorant symbols; but still in something to be fought. They at least read things in black and white, and saw life as the battlefield it is. But you are unhappy because you disbelieve in evil, and think it philosophical to see everything in the same light of grey. And I speak to you thus tonight; because tonight you have had an awakening. You saw something worthy of hate and you were happy. A mere murder might not have done it. If it had been some old man about town, or even some young man about town, it might never have touched the nerve. But I know what you felt; there was something shameful beyond speech in the death of that poor clumsy country cousin."

Noel nodded. "I think it was the shape of his coat-tails," he said.

"I thought so," answered Gale. "Well, that is the road to reality. Good night."

And he continued his walk along the suburban road, unconsciously taking in the new tint of the lawns by moonlight. But he did not see any more peacocks; and it may be accounted probable that he did not want to see any.

VII

The Purple Jewel

Gabriel Gale was a painter and poet; he was the last person to pretend to be even a very private detective. It happened that he had solved several mysteries; but most of them were the sort of mysteries more attractive to a mystic. Nevertheless, it also happened once or twice that he had to step out of the clouds of mysticism into the more brisk and bracing atmosphere of murder. Sometimes he succeeded in showing that a murder was a suicide, sometimes that a suicide was a murder; sometimes he was even involved in the study of lighter occupations like forgery and fraud. But the connexion was generally a coincidence; it concerned some point at which his imaginative interest in men's strange motives and moods happened to lead him, or at any rate them, across the border-line of legality. And in most cases, as he himself pointed out, the motives of murderers and thieves are perfectly sane and even conventional.

"I am no good at such a sensible job," he would say. "The police could easily make me look a fool in any practical matter such as they discuss in detective stories. What is the good of asking me to measure the marks made by somebody's feet all over the ground, to show why he was walking about, or where he was going? If you will show me the marks of somebody's hands all over the ground, I will tell you why he was walking upside down. But I shall find it out in the only way I ever do find out anything. And that is simply because I am mad, too, and often do it myself."

A similar brotherhood in folly probably led him into the very baffling mystery of the disappearance of Phineas Salt, the famous author and dramatist. Some of the parties involved may have accepted the parallel of setting a thief to catch a thief, when they set a poet to find a poet. For the problem did involve, in all probability, some of the purely poetical motives of a poet. And even practical people admitted that these might possibly be more familiar to a poet than to a policeman.

Phineas Salt was the sort of man whose private life was rather a public life; like that of Byron or D'Annunzio. He was a remarkable man, and perhaps rather remarkable than respectable. But there was much to be really admired in him; and there were of course any number of people who admired even what was not so admirable. The pessimistic critics claimed him as a great pessimist; and this was widely quoted in support of the theory that his disappearance was in fact a suicide. But the optimistic critics had always obstinately maintained that he was a True Optimist (whatever that may be) and these in their natural rosy rapture of optimism, dwelt rather on the idea that he had been murdered. So lurid and romantic had his whole career been made in the eyes of all Europe, that very few people kept their heads enough to reflect, or summoned their courage to suggest, that there is no particular principle in the nature of things to prevent a great poet falling down a well or being attacked by cramp while swimming at Felixstowe. Most of his admirers, and all those who were by profession journalists, preferred more sublime solutions.

He left no family, of the regular sort, except a brother in a small commercial way in the Midlands, with whom he had had very little to do; but he left a number of other people who stood to him in conspicuous spiritual or economic relations. He left a publisher, whose emotions were of mingled grief and hope in the cessation of his production of books and the high-class advertisement given to those already produced. The publisher was himself a man of considerable social distinction, as such distinctions go today; a certain Sir Walter Drummond, the head of a famous and well-established firm; and a type of a certain kind of successful Scotchman who contradicts the common tradition by combining being business-like with being extremely radiant and benevolent. He left a theatrical manager in the very act of launching his great poetical play about Alexander and the Persians; this was an artistic but adaptable Jew, named Isidore Marx, who was similarly balanced between the advantages and disadvantages of an inevitable silence following the cry of "Author". He left a beautiful but exceedingly bad-tempered leading actress, who was about to gain fresh glory in the part of the Persian Princess; and who was one of the persons not indeed few, with whom (as the quaint phrase goes) his name had been connected. He left a number of literary friends; some at least of whom were really literary and a few of whom had really been friendly. But his career had been itself so much like a sensational drama on the stage that it was surprising, when it came to real calculations about his probable conduct, how little anybody seemed to know about the essentials of his real character. And without any such clue, the circumstances seemed to make the poet's absence as disturbing and revolutionary as his presence.

Gabriel Gale, who also moved in the best literary circles, knew all this side of Phineas Salt well enough. He also had been in literary negotiations with Sir Walter Drummond. He also had been approached for poetical plays by Mr Isidore Marx. He had managed to avoid having "his name connected" with Miss Hertha Hathaway, the great Shakespearean actress; but he knew her well enough, in a world where everybody knows everybody. But being somewhat carelessly familiar with these noisy outer courts of the fame of Phineas, it gave him a mild shock of irony to pass into the more private and prosaic interior.

He owed his connexion with the case, not to this general knowledge he shared with the world of letters, but to the accident that his friend, Dr Garth, had been the family physician of the Salts. And he could not but be amused, when he attended a sort of family council of the matter, to discover how very domestic and even undistinguished the family council was; and how different from the atmosphere of large rumour and loose reputation that roared like a great wind without. He had to remind himself that it is only natural, after all, that anybody's private affairs should be private. It was absurd to expect that a wild poet would have a wild solicitor or a strange and fantastic doctor or dentist. But Dr Garth, in the very professional black suit he always wore, looked such a very family physician. The solicitor looked such a very family solicitor. He was a square-faced, silver-haired gentleman named Gunter; it seemed impossible that his tidy legal files and strongboxes could contain such material as the prolonged scandal of Phineas Salt. Joseph Salt, the brother of Phineas Salt, come up specially from the provinces, seemed so very provincial. It was hard to believe that this silent, sandy-haired, big, embarrassed tradesman, in his awkward clothes, was the one other remaining representative of such a name. The party was completed by Salt's secretary, who also seemed disconcertingly secretarial to be closely connected with such an incalculable character. Again Gale had to remind himself that even poets can only go mad on condition that a good many people connected with them remain sane. He reflected, with a faint and dawning interest, that Byron probably had a butler; and possibly even a good butler. The disconnected fancy crossed his mind that even Shelley may have gone to the dentist. He also reflected that Shelley's dentist was probably rather like any other dentist.

Nevertheless, he did not lose the sense of contrast in stepping into this inner chamber of immediate and practical responsibilities. He felt rather out of place in it; for he had no illusions about himself as a business adviser, or one to settle

139

things with the private secretary and the family lawyer. Garth had asked him to come, and he sat patiently looking at Garth; while Gunter, the solicitor, laid the general state of things before the informal committee.

"Mr Hatt has been telling us," said the lawyer, glancing for a moment at the secretary who sat opposite, "that he last saw Mr Phineas Salt at his own flat two hours after lunch on Friday last. Until about an hour ago, I should have said that this interview (which was apparently very short) was the last occasion on which the missing man had been seen. Rather more than an hour ago, however, I was rung up by a person, a complete stranger to me, who declared that he had been with Phineas Salt for the six or seven hours following on that meeting at the flat and that he was coming round to this office as soon as possible, to lay all the facts before us. This evidence, if we find it in any way worthy of credit, will at least carry the story a considerable stage further and perhaps provide us with some important hint about Mr Salt's whereabouts or fate. I do not think we can say much more about it until he comes."

"I rather fancy he has come," said Dr Garth. "I heard somebody answering the door; and that sounds like boots scaling these steep legal stairs;" for they had met in the solicitor's office in Lincoln's Inn.

The next moment a slim, middle-aged man slipped rather than stepped into the room; there was indeed something smooth and unobtrusive about the very look of his quiet grey suit, at once shabby and shiny and yet carrying something like the last glimmer of satin and elegance. The only other seizable thing about him was that he not only had rather long dark hair parted down the middle, but his long olive face was fringed with a narrow dark beard, which was also parted in the middle, drooping in two separated strands. But as he entered he laid on a chair a soft black hat with a very large brim and a very low crown; which somehow called up instantly to the fancy the cafés and the coloured lights of Paris.

"My name is James Florence," he said in a cultivated accent. "I was a very old friend of Phineas Salt; and in our younger days I have often travelled about Europe with him. I have every reason to believe that I travelled with him on his last journey."

"His last journey," repeated the lawyer, looking at him with frowning attention; "are you prepared to say that Mr Salt is dead, or are you saying this for sensationalism?"

"Well, he is either dead or something still more sensational," said Mr James Florence.

"What do you mean?" asked the other sharply. "What could be more sensational than his death?"

The stranger looked at him with a fixed and very grave expression and then said simply: "I cannot imagine."

Then, when the lawyer made an angry movement, as if suspecting a joke, the man added equally gravely: "I am still trying to imagine."

"Well," said Gunter, after a pause, "perhaps you had better tell your story and we will put the conversation on a regular footing. As you probably know, I am Mr Salt's legal adviser; this is his brother, Mr Joseph Salt, whom I am advising also; this is Dr Garth, his medical adviser. This is Mr Gabriel Gale."

The stranger bowed to the company and took a seat with quiet confidence.

"I called on my old friend Salt last Friday afternoon about five o'clock. I think I saw this gentleman leaving the flat as I came in." He looked across at the secretary, Mr Hatt, a hard-faced and reticent man, who concealed with characteristic discretion, the American name of Hiram; but could not quite conceal a certain American keenness about the look of his long chin and his spectacles. He regarded the newcomer with a face of wood, and said nothing as usual.

"When I entered the flat, I found Phineas in a very disordered and even violent condition, even for him. In fact somebody seemed to have been breaking the furniture; a statuette was knocked off its pedestal and a bowl of irises upset; and he was striding up and down the room like a roaring lion with his red mane rampant and his beard a bonfire. I thought it might be merely an artistic mood, a fine shade of poetical feeling; but he told me he had been entertaining a lady. Miss Hertha Hathaway, the actress, had only just left."

"Here, wait a minute," interposed the solicitor. "It would appear that Mr Hatt, the secretary, had also only just left. But I don't think you said anything about a lady, Mr Hatt."

"It's a pretty safe rule," said the impenetrable Hiram. "You never asked me about any lady. I've got my own work to do and I told you how I left when I'd done it."

"This is rather important, though," said Gunter doubtfully. "If Salt and the actress threw bowls and statues at each other – well, I suppose we may cautiously conclude there was some slight difference of opinion."

"There was a final smash-up," said Florence frankly. "Phineas told me he was through with all that sort of thing and, as far as I could make out, with everything else as well. He was in a pretty wild state; I think he had been drinking a little already; then he routed out a dusty old bottle of absinthe and said that he and I must drink it again in memory of old days in Paris; for it was the last time, or the last day, or some expression of that sort. Well, I hadn't drunk it myself for a long time; but I knew enough about it to know that he was drinking a great deal too much, and it's not a thing like ordinary wine or brandy; the state it can get you into is quite extraordinary; more like the clear madness that comes from hashish. And he finally rushed out of the house with that green fire in his brain and began to get out his car; starting it quite correctly and even driving it well, for there is a lucidity in such intoxication; but driving it faster and faster down the dreary vistas of the Old Kent Road and out into the country towards the south-east. He had dragged me with him with the same sort of hypnotic energy and uncanny conviviality; but I confess I felt pretty uncomfortable spinning out along the country roads with twilight turning to dark. We were nearly

killed several times; but I don't think he was trying to be killed
– at least not there on the road by an ordinary motor accident.
For he kept on crying out that he wanted the high and perilous
places of the earth; peaks and precipices and towers; that he
would like to take his last leap from some such pinnacle and
either fly like an eagle or fall like a stone. And all that seemed
the more blind and grotesque because we were driving further
and further into some of the flattest country in England, where
he certainly would never find any mountains such as towered
and toppled in his dream. And then, after I don't know how
many hours, he gave a new sort of cry; and I saw, against the last
grey strip of the gloaming and all the flat land towards the east,
the towers of Canterbury."

"I wonder," said Gabriel Gale suddenly, like a man coming
out of a dream, "how they did upset the statuette. Surely the
woman threw it, if anybody did. He'd hardly have done a thing
like that, even if he was drunk."

Then he turned his head slowly and stared rather blankly at
the equally blank face of Mr Hatt; but he said no more and,
after a slightly impatient silence, the man called Florence went
on with his narrative.

"Of course I knew that the moment he saw the great Gothic
towers of the cathedral they would mingle with his waking
nightmare and in a way fulfil and crown it. I cannot say whether
he had taken that road in order to reach the cathedral; or
whether it was merely a coincidence; but there was naturally
nothing else in all that landscape that could so fit in with his
mood about steep places and dizzy heights. And so of course he
took up his crazy parable again and talked about riding upon
gargoyles, as upon demon horses, or hunting with hellhounds
above the winds of heaven. It was very late before we reached
the cathedral; and though it stands more deeply embedded in
the town than is common in cathedral cities, it so happened
that the houses nearest to us were all barred and silent and we
stood in a deep angle of the building, which had something of

seclusion and was covered with the vast shadow of the tower. For a strong moon was already brightening behind the cathedral and I remember the light of it made a sort of ring in Salt's ragged red hair like a dull crimson fire. It seemed a rather unholy halo; and it is a detail I remember the more, because he himself was declaiming in praise of moonshine and especially of the effect of stained-glass windows seen against the moon rather than the sun, as in the famous lines in Keats. He was wild to get inside the building and see the coloured glass, which he swore was the only really successful thing religion ever did; and when he found the cathedral was locked up (as was not unusual at that hour) he had a grand final reaction of rage and scorn and began to curse the dean and chapter and everyone else. Then a blast of boyish historical reminiscence seemed to sweep through his changing mind; and he caught up a great ragged stone from the border of the turf and struck thunderous blows on the door with it, as with a hammer, and shouted aloud, 'King's men! King's men! Where is the traitor? We have come to kill the archbishop.' Then he laughed groggily and said, 'Fancy killing Dr Randall Davidson... But Becket was really worth killing. He had lived, by God! He had really made the best of both worlds, in a bigger sense than they use the phrase for. Not both at once and both tamely, as the snobs do. But one at a time and both wildly and to the limit. He went clad in crimson and gold and gained laurels and overthrew great knights in tournaments; and then suddenly became a saint, giving his goods to the poor, fasting, dying a martyr. Ah, that is the right way to do it! The right way to live a Double Life! No wonder miracles were worked at his tomb.' Then he hurled the heavy flint from him: and suddenly all the laughter and historical rant seemed to die out of his face and to leave it rather sad and sober; and as stony as one of the stone faces carved above the Gothic doors. 'I shall work a miracle tonight,' he said stolidly, 'after I have died.'

"I asked him what in the world he meant; and he made no answer. But he began abruptly to talk to me in quite a quiet and friendly and even affectionate way; thanking me for my companionship on this and many occasions; and saying that we must part; for his time was come. But when I asked him where he was going, he only pointed a finger upwards; and I could not make out at all whether he meant metaphorically that he was going to heaven or materially that he was going to scale the high tower. Anyhow, the only stairway for scaling it was inside and I could not imagine how he could reach it. I tried to question him and he answered, 'I shall ascend...; I shall be lifted up...but no miracles will be worked at my tomb. For my body will never be found.'

"And then, before I could move, and without a gesture of warning, he leapt up and caught a stone bracket by the gateway; in another second he was astride it; in a third standing on it; and in a fourth vanished utterly in the vast shadow of the wall above. Once again I heard his voice, much higher up and even far away, crying, 'I shall ascend.' Then all was silence and solitude. I cannot undertake to say whether he did ascend. I can only say with tolerable certainty that he did not descend."

"You mean," said Gunter gravely, "that you have never seen him since."

"I mean," answered James Florence equally gravely, "that I doubt whether anybody on earth has seen him since."

"Did you make inquiries on the spot?" pursued the lawyer.

The man called Florence laughed in a rather embarrassed fashion. "The truth is," he said, "that I knocked up the neighbours and even questioned the police; and I couldn't get anybody to believe me. They said I had had something to drink, which was true enough; and I think they fancied I had seen myself double, and was trying to chase my own shadow over the cathedral roofs. I dare say they know better now there has been a hue and cry in the newspapers. As for me, I took the last train back to London."

"What about the car?" asked Garth, sharply; and a light of wonder or consternation came over the stranger's face.

"Why, hang it all!" he cried. "I forgot all about poor Salt's car! We left it backed into a crack between two old houses just by the cathedral. I never thought of it again till this minute."

Gunter got up from his desk and went into the inner room, in which he was heard obscurely telephoning. When he came back, Mr Florence had already picked up his round black hat in his usual unembarrassed manner and suggested that he had better be going; for he had told all that he knew about the affair. Gunter watched him walking away with an interested expression; as if he were not quite so certain of the last assertion as he would like to be. Then he turned to the rest of the company and said:

"A curious yarn. A very curious yarn. But there's another curious thing you ought to know, that may or may not be connected with it." For the first time he seemed to take notice of the worthy Joseph Salt, who was present as the nearest surviving relative of the deceased or disappearing person. "Do you happen to know, Mr Salt, what was your brother's exact financial position?"

"I don't," said the provincial shopkeeper shortly, and contrived to convey an infinite degree of distance and distaste. "Of course you understand, gentlemen, that I'm here to do anything I can for the credit of the family. I wish I could feel quite certain that finding poor Phineas will be for the credit of the family. He and I hadn't much in common, as you may imagine; and to tell the truth, all these newspaper stories don't do a man like me very much good. Men may admire a poet for drinking green fire or trying to fly from a church tower; but they don't order their lunch from a pastry-cook's shop kept by his brother; they get a fancy there might be a little too much green fire in the ginger-ale. And I've only just opened my shop in Croydon; that is, I've bought a new business there. Also," and he looked down at the table with an embarrassment rather rustic but not unmanly, "I'm engaged to be married; and the young lady is very active in church work."

Garth could not suppress a smile at the incongruous lives of the two brothers; but he saw that there was, after all, a good deal of commonsense in the more obscure brother's attitude.

"Yes," he said, "I quite see that; but you can hardly expect the public not to be interested."

"The question I wanted to ask," said the solicitor, "has a direct bearing on something I have just discovered. Have you any notion, even a vague one, of what Phineas Salt's income was, or if he had any capital?"

"Well," said Joseph Salt reflectively, "I don't think he really had much capital; he may have had the five thousand we each of us got from the old dad's business. In fact, I think he had; but I think he lived up to the edge of his income and a bit beyond. He sometimes made big scoops on a successful play or so; but you know the sort of fellow he was; and the big scoop went in a big splash. I should guess he had two or three thousand in the bank when he disappeared."

"Quite so," said the solicitor gravely. "He had two thousand five hundred in the bank on the day he disappeared. And he drew it all out on the day he disappeared. And it entirely disappeared on the day he disappeared."

"Do you think he's bolted to foreign climes or something?" asked the brother.

"Ah," answered the lawyer, "he may have done so. Or he may have intended to do so and not done so."

"Then how did the money disappear?" asked Garth.

"It may have disappeared," replied Gunter, "while Phineas was drunk and talking nonsense to a rather shady Bohemian acquaintance, with a remarkable gift of narration."

Garth and Gale both glanced sharply across at the speaker; and both, observant in such different ways, realized that the lawyer's face was a shade too grim to be called merely cynical.

"Ah," cried the doctor with something like a catch in his breath. "And you mean something worse than theft."

"I have no right to assert even theft," said the lawyer, without relaxing his sombre expression; "but I have a right to suspect things that go rather deep. To begin with, there is some evidence for the start of Mr Florence's story, but none for its conclusion. Mr Florence met Mr Hatt; I take it, from the absence of contradiction, that Mr Hatt also met Mr Florence."

On the poker face of Mr Hatt there was still an absence of contradiction; that might presumably be taken for confirmation.

"Indeed, I have found some evidence corroborating the story of Salt starting with Florence in the car. There is no evidence corroborating all that wild moonlight antic on the roads of Kent; and if you ask me, I think it very likely that this particular joy-ride ended in some criminal den in the Old Kent Road. I telephoned a moment ago to ask about the car left in Canterbury; and they cannot at present find traces of any such car. Above all, there is the damning fact that this fellow Florence forgot all about his imaginary car, and contradicted himself by saying that he went back by train. That alone makes me think his story is false."

"Does it?" asked Gale, looking at him with childlike wonder. "Why, that alone makes me think his story is true."

"How do you mean?" asked Gunter; "that alone?"

"Yes," said Gale; "that one detail is so true that I could almost believe the truth of all the rest, if he'd described Phineas as flying from the tower on a stone dragon."

He sat frowning and blinking for a moment and then said rather testily: "Don't you see it's just the sort of mistake that would be made by that sort of man? A shabby, impecunious man, a man who never travels far except in trains, is caught up for one wild ride in a rich friend's car, drugged into a sort of dream of absinthe, dragged into a topsy-turvy mystery like a nightmare, wakes up to find his friend caught up into the sky and everybody, in broad daylight, denying that the thing had ever happened. In that sort of chilly, empty awakening, a poor man talking to a contemptuous policemen, he would no more have remembered any responsibility for the car than if it had been a fairy chariot drawn by griffins. It was part of the dream. He would automatically fall back on his ordinary way of life and take a third-class ticket home. But he would never make such a blunder in a story he had entirely made up for himself. The instant I heard him make that howler, I knew he was telling the truth."

The others were gazing at the speaker in some mild surprise, when the telephone bell, strident and prolonged, rang in the adjoining office. Gunter got hastily to his feet and went to answer it, and for a few moments there was no sound but the faint buzz of his questions and replies. Then he came back into the room, his strong face graven with a restrained stupefaction.

"This is a most remarkable coincidence," he said; "and, I must admit, a confirmation of what you say. The police down there have found the marks of a car, with tyres and general proportions like Phineas Salt's, evidently having stood exactly where James Florence professed to have left it standing. But what is even more odd, it has gone; the tracks show it was driven off down the road to the south-east by somebody. Presumably by Phineas Salt."

"To the south-east," cried Gale, and sprang to his feet. "I thought so!"

He took a few strides up and down the room and then said: "But we mustn't go too fast. There are several things. To begin with, any fool can see that Phineas would drive to the east; it was nearly daybreak when he disappeared. Of course, in that state, he would drive straight into the sunrise. What else could one do? Then, if he was really full of that craze for crags or towers, he would find himself leaving the last towers behind and driving into flatter and flatter places; for that road leads down into Thanet. What would he do? He must make for the chalk cliffs that look down at least on sea and sand; but I fancy he would want to look down on people, too; just as he might have looked down on the people of Canterbury from the cathedral tower…I know that south-eastern road…"

Then he faced them solemnly and, like one uttering a sacred mystery, said, "Margate."

"And why?" asked the staring Garth.

"A form of suicide, I suppose," said the solicitor dryly. "What could a man of that sort want to do at Margate except commit suicide?"

"What could any man want at Margate except suicide?" asked Dr Garth, who had a prejudice against such social resorts.

"A good many millions of God's images go there simply for fun," said Gale; "but it remains to be shown why one of them should be Phineas Salt…there are possibilities those black crawling masses seen from the white cliffs might be a sort of vision for a pessimist; possibly a dreadful destructive vision of shutting the gates in the cliffs and inundating them all in the ancient awful sea…or could he have some cranky notion of making Margate glorious by his creative or destructive acts; changing the very sound of the name, making it heroic or tragic for ever? There have been such notions in such men… but wherever this wild road leads, I am sure it ends in Margate."

The worthy tradesman of Croydon was the first to get to his feet after Gale had risen, and he fingered the lapels of his outlandish coat with all his native embarrassment. "I'm afraid all this is beyond me, gentlemen," he said, "gargoyles and dragons and pessimists and such are not in my line. But it does seem that the police have got a clue that points down the Margate road; and if you ask me, I think we'd better discuss this matter again when the police have investigated a little more."

"Mr Salt is perfectly right," said the lawyer heartily. "See what it is to have a business man to bring us back to business. I will go and make some more inquiries; and soon, perhaps, I may have a little more to tell you."

If Gabriel Gale was, and felt himself to be, an incongruous figure in the severe framework of leather and parchment, of law and commerce, represented by the office of Mr Gunter, it might well have been supposed that he would feel even more of a fish out of water in the scene of the second family council. For it was held at the new headquarters of the family, or all that remained of the family; the little shop in Croydon over which the lost poet's very prosaic brother was presiding with a mixture of the bustle of a new business and the last lingering formalities of a funeral. Mr J Salt's suburban shop was a very suburban shop. It was a shop for selling confectionery and sweetmeats and similar things; with a sort of side-show of very mild refreshments, served on little round shiny tables and apparently chiefly consisting of pale green lemonade. The cakes and sweets were arranged in decorative patterns in the window, to attract the eye of Croydon youth, and as the building consisted chiefly of windows, it seemed full of a sort of cold and discolouring light. A parlour behind, full of neat but illogical knicknacks and momentoes, was not without a sampler, a testimonial from a Provident Society and a portrait of George V. But it was never easy to predict in what place or circumstances Mr Gale would find a certain intellectual interest. He generally looked at objects, not objectively in the sense of seeing them as themselves, but in connexion with some curious trains of thought of his own; and, for some reason or other, he seemed to take quite a friendly interest in Mr Salt's suburban shop. Indeed, he seemed to take more interest in this novel scene than in the older and more serious problem which he had come there to solve. He gazed entranced at the china dogs and pink pincushions on the parlour mantelpiece; he was with difficulty drawn away from a rapt contemplation of the diamond pattern of lemon drops and raspberry drops which decorated the window; and he looked even at the lemonade as if it were as important as that pale green wine of wormwood, which had apparently played a real part in the tragedy of Phineas Salt.

He had been indeed unusually cheerful all the morning, possibly because it was a beautiful day, possibly for more personal reasons; and had drawn near to the rendezvous through the trim suburban avenues with a step of unusual animation. He saw the worthy confectioner himself, stepping out of a villa of a social shade faintly superior to his own; a young woman with a crown of braided brown hair, and a good grave face, came with him down the garden path. Gale had little difficulty in identifying the young lady interested in church work. The poet gazed at the pale squares of lawn and the few thin and dwarfish trees with quite a sentimental interest, almost as if it were a romance of his own; nor did his universal good humour fail him even when he encountered, a few lamp-posts further down the road, the saturnine and somewhat unsympathetic countenance of Mr Hiram Hatt. The lover was still lingering at the garden gate, after the fashion of his kind, and Hatt and Gale walked more briskly ahead of him towards his home. To Hatt the poet made the somewhat irrelevant remark: "Do you understand that desire to be one of the lovers of Cleopatra?"

Mr Hatt, the secretary, indicated that, had he nourished such a desire, his appearance on the historical scene would have lacked something of true American hustle and punctuality.

"Oh, there are plenty of Cleopatras still," answered Gale; "and plenty of people who have that strange notion of being the hundredth husband of an Egyptian cat. What could have made a man of real intellect, like that fellow's brother, break himself all up for a woman like Hertha Hathaway?"

"Well, I'm all with you there," said Hatt. "I didn't say anything about the woman, because it wasn't my business; but I tell you, sir, she was just blue ruin and vitriol. Only the fact that I didn't mention her seems to have set your friend the solicitor off on another dance of dark suspicions. I swear he fancies she and I were mixed up in something; and probably had to do with the disappearance of Phineas Salt."

Gale looked hard at the man's hard face for a moment and then said irrelevantly:

"Would it surprise you to find him at Margate?"

"No; nor anywhere else," replied Hatt. "He was restless just then and drifted about into the commonest crowds. He did no work lately; sometimes sat and stared at a blank sheet of paper as if he had no ideas."

"Or as if he had too many," said Gabriel Gale.

With that they turned in at the confectioner's door: and found Dr Garth already in the outer shop, having only that moment arrived. But when they penetrated to the parlour, they came on a figure that gave them, indescribably, a cold shock of sobriety. The lawyer was already seated in that gimcrack room, resolutely and rather rudely, with his top hat on his head, like a bailiff in possession; but they all sensed something more sinister, as of the bearer of the bowstring.

"Where is Mr Joseph Salt?" he asked. "He said he would be home at eleven."

Gale smiled faintly and began to fiddle with the funny little ornaments on the mantelpiece. "He is saying farewell," he said. "Sometimes it is rather a long word to say."

"We must begin without him," said Gunter. "Perhaps it is just as well."

"You mean you have bad news for him?" asked the doctor, lowering his voice. "Have you the last news of his brother?"

"I believe it may fairly be called the last news," answered the lawyer dryly. "In the light of the latest discoveries – Mr Gale, I should be much obliged if you would leave off fidgeting with those ornaments and sit down. There is something that somebody has got to explain."

"Yes," replied Gale rather hazily. "Isn't *this* what he has got to explain?"

He picked up something from the mantelpiece and put it on the central table. It was a very absurd object to be stared at thus, as an exhibit in a grim museum of suicide or crime. It was a cheap, childish, pink and white mug, inscribed in large purple letters, "A Present from Margate".

"There is a date inside," said Gale, looking down dreamily into the depths of this remarkable receptacle. "This year. And we're still at the beginning of the year, you know."

"Well, it may be one of the things," said the solicitor. "But I have got some other Presents from Margate."

He took a sheaf of papers from his breast pocket and laid them out thoughtfully on the table before he spoke.

"Understand, to begin with, that there really is a riddle and the man really has vanished. Don't imagine a man can easily melt into a modern crowd; the police have traced his car on the road and could have traced him, if he had left it. Don't imagine anybody can simply drive down country roads throwing corpses out of cars. There are always a lot of fussy people about, who notice a little thing like that. Whatever he did, sooner or later the explanation would probably be found; and we have found it."

Gale put down the mug abruptly and stared across, still open-mouthed, but as it were more dry-throated, coughing and stammering now with a real eagerness.

"Have you really found out?" he asked. "Do you know all about the Purple Jewel?"

"Look here!" cried the doctor, as if with a generous indignation; "this is getting too thick. I don't mind being in a mystery, but it needn't be a melodrama. Don't say that we are after the Rajah's Ruby. Don't say, oh, don't say, that it is in the eye of the god Vishnu."

"No," replied the poet. "It is in the eye of the Beholder."

"And who's he?" asked Gunter. "I don't know exactly what you're talking about, but there may have been a theft involved. Anyhow, there was more than a theft."

He sorted out from his papers two or three photographs of the sort that are taken casually with hand cameras in a holiday crowd. As he did so he said: "Our investigations at Margate have not been fruitless; in fact they have been rather fruitful. We have found a witness, a photographer on Margate beach, who testifies to having seen a man corresponding to Phineas Salt, burly and with a big red beard and long hair, who stood for some time on an isolated crag of white chalk, which stands out from the cliff, and looked down at the crowds below. Then he descended by a rude stairway cut in the chalk and, crossing a crowded part of the beach, spoke to another man who seemed to be an ordinary clerk or commonplace holidaymaker; and, after a little talk, they went up to the row of bathing-sheds, apparently for the purpose of having a dip in the sea. My informant thinks they did go into the sea; but cannot be quite so certain. What he is quite certain of is that he never saw the red-bearded man again, though he did see the commonplace clean-shaven man, both when he returned in his bathing-suit and when he resumed his ordinary, his very ordinary, clothes. He not only saw him, but he actually took a snapshot of him, and there he is."

He handed the photograph to Garth, who gazed at it with slowly rising eyebrows. The photograph represented a sturdy man with a bulldog jaw but rather blank eyes, with his head lifted, apparently staring out to sea. He wore very light holiday clothes, but of a clumsy, unfashionable cut; and, so far as he could be seen under the abrupt shadow and rather too jaunty angle of his stiff straw hat, his hair was of some light colour. Only, as it happened, the doctor had no need to wait for the development of colour photography. For he knew exactly what colour it was. He knew it was a sort of sandy red; he had often seen it, not in the photograph, but on the head where it grew. For the man in the stiff straw hat was most unmistakably Mr Joseph Salt, the worthy confectioner and new social ornament to the suburb of Croydon.

"So Phineas went down to Margate to meet his brother," said Garth. "After all, that's natural enough in one way. Margate is exactly the sort of place his brother would go to."

"Yes; Joseph went there on one of those motor-charabanc expeditions, with a whole crowd of other trippers, and he seems to have returned the same night on the same vehicle. But nobody knows when, where or *if* his brother Phineas returned."

"I rather gather from your tone," said Garth very gravely, "that you think his brother Phineas never did return."

"I think his brother never will return," said the lawyer, "unless it happens (by a curious coincidence) that he was drowned while bathing and his body is someday washed up on the shore. But there's a strong current running just there that would carry it far away."

"The plot thickens, certainly," said the doctor. "All this bathing business seems to complicate things rather."

"I am afraid," said the lawyer, "that it simplifies them very much."

"What," asked Garth sharply. "Simplifies?"

"Yes," said the other, gripping the arms of his chair and rising abruptly to his feet. "I think this story is as simple as the story of Cain and Abel. And rather like it."

There was a shocked silence, which was at length broken by Gale, who was peering into the Present from Margate, crying or almost crowing, in the manner of a child.

"Isn't it a funny little mug! He must have bought it before he came back in the charabanc. Such a jolly thing to buy, when you have just murdered your own brother."

"It does seem a queer business," said Dr Garth frowning. "I suppose one might work out some explanation of how he did it. I suppose a man might drown another man while they were bathing, even off a crowded beach like that. But I'm damned if I can understand why he did it. Have you discovered a motive as well as a murder?"

"The motive is old enough and I think obvious enough," answered Gunter. "We have in this case all the necessary elements of a hatred, of that slow and corroding sort that is founded on jealousy. Here you had two brothers, sons of the same insignificant Midland tradesman; having the same education environment, opportunities; very nearly of an age, very much of one type, even of one physical type, rugged, red-haired, rather plain and heavy, until Phineas made himself a spectacle with that big Bolshevist beard and bush of hair; not so different in youth but that they must have had ordinary rivalries and quarrels on fairly equal terms. And then see the sequel. One of them fills the world with his name, wears a laurel like the crown of Petrach, dines with kings and emperors and is worshipped by women like a hero on the films. The other – isn't it enough to say that the other has had to go on slaving all his life in a room like this?"

"Don't you like the room?" inquired Gale with the same simple eagerness. "Why, I think some of the ornaments are so nice!"

"It is not yet quite clear," went on Gunter, ignoring him, "how the pastry-cook lured the poet down to Margate and a dip in the sea. But the poet was admittedly rather random in his movements just then, and too restless to work; and we have no reason to suppose that he knew of the fraternal hatred or that he in any way reciprocated it. I don't think there would be much difficulty in swimming with a man beyond the crowd of bathers and holding him under water, till you could send his body adrift on a current flowing away from the shore. Then he went back and dressed and calmly took his place in the charabanc."

"Don't forget the dear little mug," said Gale softly. "He stopped to buy that and then went home. Well, it's a very able and thorough explanation and reconstruction of the crime, my dear Gunter, and I congratulate you. Even the best achievements have some little flaw; and there's only one trifling mistake in yours. You've got it the wrong way round."

"What do you mean?" asked the other quickly.

"Quite a small correction," explained Gale. "You think that Joseph was jealous of Phineas. As a matter of fact, Phineas was jealous of Joseph."

"My dear Gale, you are simply playing the goat," said the doctor very sharply and impatiently. "And let me tell you I don't think it's a decent occasion for doing it. I know all about your jokes and fancies and paradoxes, but we're all in a damned hard position, sitting here in the man's own house, and knowing we're in the house of a murderer."

"I know – it's simply infernal," said Gunter, his stiffness shaken for the first time; and he looked up with a shrinking jerk, as if he half expected to see the rope hanging from that dull and dusty ceiling.

At the same moment the door was thrown open and the man they had convicted of murder stood in the room. His eyes were bright like a child's over a new toy, his face was flushed to the roots of his fiery hair, his broad shoulders were squared backwards like a soldier's; and in the lapel of his coat was a large purple flower, of a colour that Gale remembered in the garden-beds of the house down the road. Gale had no difficulty in guessing the reason of this triumphant entry.

Then the man with the buttonhole saw the tragic faces on the other side of the table and stopped, staring.

"Well," he said at last, in a rather curious tone. "What about your search?"

The lawyer was about to open his locked lips with some such question as was once asked of Cain by the voice out of the cloud, when Gale interrupted him by flinging himself backwards in a chair and emitting a short but cheery laugh.

"I've given up the search," said Gale gaily. "No need to bother myself about that any more."

"Because you know you will never find Phineas Salt," said the tradesman steadily.

"Because I have found him," said Gabriel Gale.

Dr Garth got to his feet quickly and remained staring at them with bright eyes.

"Yes," said Gale, "because I am talking to him." And he smiled across at his host, as if he had just been introduced.

Then he said rather more gravely: "Will you tell us all about it, Mr Phineas Salt? Or must I guess it for you all the way through?"

There was a heavy silence.

"You tell the story," said the shopkeeper at last. "I am quite sure you know all about it."

"I only know about it," answered Gale gently, "because I think I should have done the same thing myself. It's what some call having a sympathy with lunatics – including literary men."

"Hold on for a moment," interposed the staring Mr Gunter. "Before you get too literary, am I to understand that this gentleman, who owns this shop, actually is the poet, Phineas Salt? In that case, where is his brother?"

"Making the Grand Tour, I imagine," said Gale. "Gone abroad for a holiday, anyhow; a holiday which will be not the less enjoyable for the two thousand five hundred pounds that his brother gave him to enjoy himself with. His slipping away was easy enough; he only swam a little bit further along the shore to where they had left another suit of clothes. Meanwhile our friend here went back and shaved off his beard and effected the change of appearance in the bathing-tent. He was quite sufficiently like his brother to go back with a crowd of strangers. And then, you will doubtless note, he opened a new shop in an entirely new neighbourhood."

"But *why?*" cried Garth in a sort of exasperation. "In the name of all the saints and angels, why? That's what I can't make any sense of."

"I will tell you why," said Gabriel Gale, "but you won't make any sense of it."

He stared at the mug on the table for a moment and then said: "This is what you would call a nonsense story; and you can only understand it by understanding nonsense; or, as some politely call it, poetry. The poet Phineas Salt was a man who had made himself master of everything, in a sort of frenzy of freedom and omnipotence. He had tried to feel everything, experience everything, imagine everything that could be or could not be. And he found, as all such men have found, that that illimitable liberty is itself a limit. It is like the circle, which is at once an eternity and a prison. He not only wanted to do everything. He wanted to be everybody. To the Pantheist God is everybody: to the Christian He is also somebody. But this sort of Pantheist will not narrow himself by a choice. To want everything is to will nothing. Mr Hatt here told me that Phineas would sit staring at a blank sheet of paper; and I told him it was not because he had nothing to write about, but because he could write about anything. When he stood on that cliff and looked down on that mazy crowd, so common and yet so complex, he felt he could write ten thousand tales and then that he could write none; because there was no reason to choose one more than another.

"Well, what is the step beyond that? What comes next? I tell you there are only two steps possible after that. One is the step over the cliff; to cease to be. The other is to *be* somebody, instead of writing about everybody. It is to become incarnate as one real human being in that crowd; to begin all over again as a real person. Unless a man be born again –

"He tried it and found that this was what he wanted; the things he had not known since childhood; the silly little lower middle-class things; to have to do with lollipops and ginger beer; to fall in love with a girl round the corner and feel awkward about it; to be young. That was the only paradise still left virgin and unspoilt enough, in the imagination of a man who has turned the seven heavens upside down. That is what he tried as his last experiment, and I think we can say it has been a success."

"Yes," said the confectioner with a stony satisfaction, "it has been a great success."

Mr Gunter, the solicitor, rose also with a sort of gesture of despair. "Well, I don't think I understand it any better for knowing all about it," he said; "but I suppose it must be as you say. But how in the world did you know it yourself?"

"I think it was those coloured sweets in the window that set me off," said Gale. "I couldn't take my eyes off them. They were so pretty. Sweets are better than jewellery: the children are right. For they have the fun of eating rubies and emeralds. I felt sure they were speaking to me in some way. And then I realized what they were saying. Those violet or purple raspberry drops were as vivid and glowing as amethysts, when you saw them from *inside* the shop; but from outside, with the light on them, they would look quite dingy and dark. Meanwhile, there were plenty of other things, gilded or painted with opaque colours, that would have looked much more gay in the shop window, to the customer looking in at it. Then I remembered the man who said he must break into the cathedral to see the coloured windows from inside, and I knew it in an instant. The man who had arranged that shop window was not a shopkeeper. He was not thinking of how things looked from the street, but of how they looked to his own artistic eye from inside. From there he saw purple jewels. And then, thinking of the cathedral, of course I remembered something else. I remembered what the poet had said about the Double Life of St Thomas of Canterbury; and how when he had all the earthly glory, he had to have the exact opposite. St Phineas of Croydon is also living a Double Life."

"Well," broke out Gunter, heaving with a sort of heavy gasp, "with all respect to him, if he has done all this, I can only say that he must have gone mad."

"No," said Gale, "a good many of my friends have gone mad and I am by no means without sympathy with them. But you can call this the story of 'The Man Who went Sane'."

VIII

THE ASYLUM OF ADVENTURE

A very small funeral procession passed through a very small churchyard on the rocky coast of Cornwall; carrying a coffin to its grave under the low and windy wall. The coffin was quite formal and unobtrusive; but the knot of fishermen and labourers eyed it with the slanted eyes of superstition; almost as if it had been the misshapen coffin of legend that was said to contain a monster. For it contained the body of a near neighbour, who had long lived a stone's throw from them, and whom they had never seen.

The figure following the coffin, the chief and only mourner, they had seen fairly often. He had a habit of disappearing into his late friend's house and being invisible for long periods, but he came and went openly. No one knew when the dead man had first come, but he probably came in the night; and he went out in the coffin. The figure following it was a tall figure in black, bareheaded, with the sea blast whistling through his wisps of yellow hair as through the pale sea grasses. He was still young and none could have said that his mourning suit sat ill upon him; but some who knew him would have seen it with involuntary surprise, and felt that it showed him in a new phase. When he was dressed, as he generally was, in the negligent tweeds and stockings of the pedestrian landscape painter, he looked merely amiable and absent-minded; but the black brought out something more angular and fixed about his face. With his black garb and yellow hair he might have been the traditional Hamlet; and indeed the look in his eyes was visionary and vague; but the traditional Hamlet would hardly have had so long and straight a chin as that which rested unconsciously on his black cravat. After the ceremony, he left the village church and walked towards the village post office, gradually lengthening and lightening his stride, like a man who, with all care for decency, can hardly conceal that he is rid of a duty.

"It's a horrible thing to say," he said to himself, "but I feel like a happy widower."

He then went in to the post office and sent off a telegram addressed to a Lady Diana Westermaine, Westermaine Abbey: a telegram that said: "I am coming tomorrow to keep my promise and tell you the story of a strange friendship."

Then he went out of the little shop again and walked eastwards out of the village, with undisguised briskness, till he had left the houses far behind, and his funeral hat and habit were an almost incongruous black spot upon great green uplands and the motley forests of autumn. He had walked for about half a day, lunched on bread and cheese and ale at a little public house, and resumed his march with unabated cheerfulness, when the first event of that strange day befell him. He was threading his way by a river that ran in a hollow of the green hills; and at one point his path narrowed and ran under a high stone wall. The wall was built of very large flat stones of ragged outline, and a row of them ran along the top like the teeth of a giant. He would not normally have taken so much notice of the structure of the wall; indeed he did not take any notice of it at all until after something had happened. Until (in fact) there was a great gap in the row of craggy teeth, and one of the crags lay flat at his feet, shaking up dust like the smoke of an explosion. It had just brushed one of his long wisps of light hair as it fell.

Looking up, a shade bewildered by the shock of his hairbreadth escape, he saw for an instant in the dark gap left in the stonework a face, peering and malignant. He called out promptly:

"I see you; I could send you to jail for that!"

"No you can't," retorted the stranger, and vanished into the twilight of trees as swiftly as a squirrel.

The gentleman in black, whose name was Gabriel Gale, looked up thoughtfully at the wall, which was rather too high and smooth to scale; besides the fugitive had already far too much of a start. Mr Gale finally said aloud, in a reflective fashion: "Now I wonder why he did that!" Then he frowned with an entirely new sort of gravity, and after a moment or two of grim silence he added: "But after all its much more odd and mysterious that he should *say* that."

In truth, though the three words uttered by the unknown person seemed trivial enough, they sufficed to lead Gale's memories backwards to the beginning of the whole business that ended in the little Cornish churchyard; and as he went briskly on his way he rehearsed all the details of that old story, which he was to tell to the lady at his journey's end.

Nearly fourteen years before, Gabriel Gale had come of age and inherited the moderate debts and the small freehold of a rather unsuccessful gentleman farmer. But though he grew up with the traditions of a sort of small squire, he was not the sort of person, especially at that age, to have no opinions except those traditions. In early youth his politics were the very reverse of squires' politics; he was very much of a revolutionary and locally rather a firebrand. He intervened on behalf of poachers and gipsies: he wrote letters to the local papers which the editors thought too eloquent to be printed. He denounced the county magistracy in controversies that had to be impartially adjudged by the county magistrates. Finding, curiously enough, that all these authorities were against him, and seemed to be in legal control of all his methods of self-expression, he invented a method of his own which gave him great amusement and the authorities great annoyance. He fell, in fact, to employing a talent for drawing and painting which he was conscious of possessing, along with another talent for guessing people's thoughts and getting a rapid grasp of their characters, which he was less conscious of possessing, but which he certainly possessed. It is a talent very valuable to a portrait painter: in this case, however, he became a rather peculiar sort of portrait painter. It was not exactly what is generally called a fashionable portrait painter. Gale's small estate contained several outhouses with whitewashed walls or palings abutting on the high road; and whenever a magnate or magistrate did anything that Gale disapproved of, Gale was in the habit of painting his portrait in public and on a large scale. His pictures were hardly in the ordinary sense caricatures, but they were the portraits of souls. There was nothing crude about the picture of the great merchant prince now honoured with a peerage; the eyes looking up from under lowered brows, the sleek hair parted low on the forehead, were hardly exaggerated; but the smiling lips were certainly saying: "And the next article?" One even knew that it was not really a very superior article. The picture of the formidable Colonel Ferrars did justice to the distinction of the face, with its frosty eyebrows and moustaches; but it also very distinctly discovered that it was the face of a fool, and of one subconsciously frightened of being found to be a fool.

With these coloured proclamations did Mr Gale beautify the countryside and make himself beloved among his equals. They could not do very much in the matter; it was not libel, for nothing was said; it was not nuisance or damage, for it was done on his own property, though in sight of the whole world. Among those who gathered every day to watch the painter at work, was a sturdy, red-faced, bushy-whiskered farmer, named

Banks, seemingly one of those people who delight in any event and are more or less impenetrable by any opinion. He never could be got to bother his head about the sociological symbolism of Gale's caricatures; but he regarded the incident with exuberant interest as one of the great stories calculated to be the glory of the country, like a calf born with five legs or some pleasant ghost story about the old gallows on the moor. Though so little of a theorist he was far from being a fool, and had a whole tangle of tales both humorous and tragic, to show how rich a humanity was packed within the four corners of his countryside. Thus it happened that he and his revolutionary neighbour had many talks over the cakes and ale, and went on many expeditions together to fascinating graves or historic public houses. And thus it happened that on one of these expeditions Banks fell in with two of his other cronies, who made a party of four, making discoveries not altogether without interest.

The first of the farmer's friends, introduced to Gale under the name of Starkey, was a lively little man with a short stubbly beard and sharp eyes, which he was in the habit however of screwing up with a quizzical smile during the greater part of a conversation. Both he and his friend Banks were eagerly interested in the story of Gale's political protests, if they regarded them only too much as practical jokes. And they were both particularly anxious to introduce a friend of theirs named Wolfe, always referred to as Sim, who had a hobby, it would seem, in such matters, and might have suggestions to make. With a sort of sleepy curiosity which was typical of him, Gale found himself trailed along in an expedition for the discovery of Sim; and Sim was discovered at a little obscure hostelry called the Grapes a mile or so up the river. The three men had taken a boat, with the small Starkey for coxswain; it was a glorious autumn morning but the river was almost hidden under high banks and overhanging woods, intersected with great gaps of glowing sunlight, in one of which the lawns of the little riverside hotel sloped down to the river. And on the bank overhanging the river a man stood waiting for them; a remarkable looking man with a fine sallow face rather like an actor's and very curly grizzled hair. He welcomed them with a pleasant smile, and then turned towards the house with something of a habit of command or at least of direction. "I've ordered something for you," he said. "If we go in now it will be ready."

As Gabriel Gale brought up the rear of the single file of four men going up the straight paved path to the inn door, his roaming eye took in the rest of the garden, and something stirred in his spirit, which was also prone to roaming, and even in a light sense to a sort of rebellion. The steep path was lined with little trees, looking like the plan of a sampler. He did not see why he should walk straight up so very straight a path, and many things in the garden took his wandering fancy. He would much rather have had lunch at one of the little weather-stained tables standing about on the lawn. He would have been delighted to grope in the dark and tumble-down arbour in the corner, of which he could dimly see the circular table and semi-circular seat in the shadow of its curtain of creepers. He was even more attracted by the accident by which an old children's swing, with its posts and ropes and hanging seat, stood close up to the bushes of the river bank. In fact, the last infantile temptation was irresistible; and calling out, "I'm going over here," he ran across the garden towards the arbour, taking the swing with a sort of leap on his way. He landed in the wooden seat and swung twice back and forth, leaving it again with another flying leap. Just as he did so, however, the rope broke at its upper attachment, and he fell all askew, kicking his legs in the air. He was on his feet again immediately, and found himself confronted by his three companions who had followed in doubt or remonstrance. But the smiling Starkey was foremost, and his screwed up eyes expressed good humour and even sympathy.

"Rotten sort of swing of yours," he said. "These things are all falling to pieces," and he gave the other rope a twitch, bringing that down also. Then he added: "Want to feast in the arbour, do you? Very well; you go in first and break the cobwebs. When you've collected all the spiders, I'll follow you."

Gale dived laughing into the dark corner in question and sat down in the centre of the crescent-shaped seat. The practical Mr Banks had apparently entirely refused to carouse in this leafy cavern; but the figures of the two other men soon darkened the entrance and they sat down, one at each horn of the crescent.

"I suppose that was a sudden impulse of yours," said the man named Wolfe, smiling. "You poets often have sudden impulses, don't you?"

"It's not for me to say it was a poet's impulse," replied Gale; "but I'm sure it would need a poet to describe it. Perhaps I'm not one; anyhow I never could describe those impulses. The only way to do it would be to write a poem about the swing and a poem about the arbour, and put them both into a longer poem about the garden. And poems aren't produced quite so quickly as all that, though I've always had a notion that a real poet would never talk prose. He would talk about the weather in rolling stanzas like the storm clouds, or ask you to pass the potatoes in an impromptu lyric as beautiful as the blue flower of the potato."

"Make it a prose poem, then," said the man whose name was Simeon Wolfe, "and tell us how you felt about the garden and the garden swing."

Gabriel Gale was both sociable and talkative; he talked a great deal about himself because he was not an egoist. He talked a great deal about himself on the present occasion. He was pleased to find these two intelligent men interested and attentive; and he tried to put into words the impalpable impulses to which he was always provoked by particular shapes or colours or corners of the straggling road of life. He tried to analyse the attraction of a swing, with its rudiments of aviation; and how it made a man feel more like a boy, because it made a boy feel more like a bird. He explained that the arbour was fascinating precisely because it was a den. He told them at some length of the psychological truth; that dismal and decayed objects raise a man's spirits higher, if they really are already high. His two companions talked in turn; and as luncheon progressed and passed they turned over between them many strange strata of personal experience, and Gale began to understand their personalities and their point of view. Wolfe had travelled a great deal, especially in the East; Starkey's experiences had been more local but equally curious, and they both had known many psychological cases and problems about which to compare notes. They both agreed that Gale's mental processes in the matter, though unusual, were not unique.

"In fact," observed Wolfe, "I think your mind belongs to a particular class, and one of which I have had some experience. Don't you think so, Starkey?"

"I quite agree," said the other man, nodding.

It was at that moment that Gale looked out dreamily at the light upon the lawn, and in the stillness of his inmost mind a light broke on him like lightning; one of the terrible intuitions of his life.

Against the silver light on the river the dark frame of the forsaken swing stood up like a gallows. There was no trace of the seat or the ropes, not merely in their proper place, but even on the ground where they had fallen. Sweeping his eye slowly and searchingly round the scene, he saw them at last, huddled and hidden in a heap behind the bench where Starkey was sitting. In an instant he understood everything. He knew the profession of the two men on each side of him. He knew why they were asking him to describe the processes of his mind. Soon they would be taking out a document and signing it. He would not leave that arbour a free man.

"So you are both doctors," he observed cheerfully, "and you both think I am mad."

"The word is really very unscientific," said Simeon Wolfe in a soothing fashion.

"You are of a certain type which friends and admirers will be wise to treat in a certain way, but it need in no sense be an unfriendly or uncomfortable way. You are an artist with that form of the artistic temperament which is necessarily a mode of modified megalomania, and which expresses itself in the form of exaggeration. You cannot see a large blank wall without having an uncontrollable appetite for covering it with large pictures. You cannot see a swing hung in the air without thinking of flying ships careering through the air. I will venture to guess that you never see a cat without thinking of a tiger or a lizard without thinking of a dragon."

"That is perfectly correct," said Gale gravely; "I never do."

Then his mouth twisted a little, as if a whimsical idea had come into his mind. "Psychology is certainly very valuable," he said. "It seems to teach us how to see into each other's minds. You, for instance, have a mind which is very interesting: you have reached a condition which I think I recognize. You are in that particular attitude in which the subject, when he thinks of anything, never thinks of the centre of anything. You see only edges eaten away. Your malady is the opposite to mine, to what you call making a tiger out of a cat, or what some call making a mountain out of a molehill. You do not go on and make a cat more of a cat; you are always trying to work back and prove that it is less than a cat; that it is a defective cat or a mentally deficient cat. But a cat is a cat; that is the supreme sanity which is so thickly clouded in your mind. After all, a molehill is a hill and a mountain is a hill. But you have got into the state of the mad queen, who said she knew hills compared with which this was a valley. You can't grasp the thing called a thing. Nothing for you has a central stalk of sanity. There is no core to your cosmos. Your trouble began with being an atheist."

"I have not confessed to being an atheist," said Wolfe staring.

"I have not confessed to being an artist," replied Gale, "or to have uncontrolled artistic appetites or any of that stuff. But I will tell you one thing: I can only exaggerate things the way they are going. But I'm not often wrong about the way they are going. You may be as sleek as a cat but I knew you were evolving into a tiger. And I guessed this little lizard could be turned by black magic into a dragon."

As he spoke he was looking grimly at Starkey and out under the dark arch of the arbour, as out of a closing prison, with these two ghouls sitting on each side of the gate. Beyond was the gaunt shape like a gallows and beyond that the green and silver of the garden and the stream shone like a lost paradise of liberty. But it was characteristic of him that even when he was practically hopeless, he liked being logically triumphant; he liked turning the tables on his critics even when, so to speak, they were as abstract as multiplication tables.

"Why, my learned friends," he went on contemptuously, "do you really suppose you are any fitter to write a report on my mind than I am on yours? You can't see any further into me than I can into you. Not half so far. Didn't you know a portrait painter has to value people at sight as much as a doctor? And I do it better than you; I have a knack that way. That's why I can paint those pictures on the wall; and I could paint your pictures as big as a house. I know what is at the back of your mind, Doctor Simeon Wolfe; and it's a chaos of exceptions with no rule. You could find anything abnormal, because you have no normal. You could find anybody mad; and as for why you specially want to find me mad – why that is another disadvantage of being an atheist. You do not think anything will smite you for the vile treachery you have sold yourself to do today."

"There is no doubt about your condition now," said Dr Wolfe with a sneer.

"You look like an actor, but you are not a very good actor," answered Gale calmly. "I can see that my guess was correct. These rack-renters and usurers who oppress the poor, in my own native valley, could not find any pettifogging law to prevent me from painting the colours of their souls in hell. So they have bribed you and another cheap doctor to certify me for a madhouse. I know the sort of man you are. I know this is not the first dirty trick you have done to help the rich out of a hole. You would do anything for your paymasters. Possibly the murder of the unborn."

Wolfe's face was still wrinkled with its Semitic sneer, but his olive tint had turned to a sort of loathsome yellow. Starkey called out with sudden shrillness, as abrupt as the bark of a dog.

"Speak more respectfully!"

"There is Dr Starkey, too," continued the poet lazily. "Let us turn our medical attention to the mental state of Dr Starkey."

As he rolled his eyes with ostentatious languor in the new direction, he was arrested by a change in the scene without. A strange man was standing under the frame of the swing, looking up at it with his head on one side like a bird's. He was a small, sturdy figure, quite conventionally clad; and Gale could only suppose he was a stray guest of the hotel. His presence did not help very much; for the law was probably on the side of the doctors; and Gale continued his address to them.

"The mental deficiency of Dr Starkey," he said, "consists in having forgotten the truth. You, Starkey, have no sceptical philosophy like your friend. You are a practical man, my dear Starkey; but you have told lies so incessantly and from so early an age that you never see anything as it is, but only as it could be made to look. Beside each thing stands the unreal thing that is its shadow; and you see the shadow first. You are very quick in seeing it; you go direct to the deceptive potentialities of anything; you see at once if anything could be used as anything else. You are the original man who went straight down the crooked lane. I could see how quickly you saw that the swing would provide ropes to tie me up if I were violent; and that going first into this arbour, I should be cornered, with you on each side of me. Yet the swing and the arbour were my own idea; and that again is typical of you. You're not a scientific thinker like the other scoundrel; you have always picked up other men's ideas, but you pick as swiftly as a pickpocket. In fact, when you see an idea sticking out of a pocket you can hardly help picking it. That's where you're mad; you can't resist being clever, or rather borrowing cleverness. Which means you have sometimes been too clever to be lucky. You are a shabbier sort of scamp; and I rather fancy you have been in prison."

Starkey sprang to his feet, snatching up the ropes and throwing them on the table.

"Tie him up and gag him," he cried; "he is raving."

"There again," observed Gale, "I enter with sympathy into your thoughts. You mean that I must be gagged at once; for if I were free for half a day, or perhaps half an hour, I could find out the facts about you and tear your reputation to rags."

As he spoke he again followed with an interested eye the movements of the strange man outside. The man had recrossed the garden, calmly picking up a chair from one of the little tables, and returned carrying it lightly in the direction of the arbour. To the surprise of all, he set it down at the round table in the very entrance of that retreat, and sat down on it with his hands in his pockets, staring at Gabriel Gale. With his face in shadow, his square head, short hair and bulk of shoulders took on a new touch of mystery.

"Hope I don't interrupt," he said. "Perhaps it would be more honest to say I hope I do interrupt. Because I want to interrupt. Honestly, I think you medical gentlemen would be very unwise to gag your friend here, or try to carry him off."

"And why?" asked Starkey sharply.

"Only because I should kill you if you did," replied the stranger.

They all stared at him; and Wolfe sneered again as he said: "You might find it awkward to kill us both at once."

The stranger took his hands out of his pockets; and with the very gesture there was a double flash of metal. For the hands held two revolvers which pointed at them, fixed them like two large fingers of steel.

"I shall only kill you if you run or call out," said the strange gentleman pleasantly.

"If you do you'll be hanged," cried Wolfe violently.

"Oh, no, I shan't," said the stranger; "not unless two dead men can get up and hang me on that nursery gallows in the garden. I'm allowed to kill people. There's a special Act of Parliament permitting me to go about killing anybody I like. I'm never punished, whatever I do. In fact, to tell you the truth, I'm the King of England, and the Constitution says I can do no wrong."

"What are you talking about?" demanded the doctor. "You must be mad."

The stranger uttered a sudden shout of laughter that shook the shed and the nerves of all three hearers.

"You've hit it first shot," he cried. "He said you were quick, didn't he? Yes, I'm mad all right; I've just escaped from the same sanatorium next door, where you want to take your friend to. I escaped in a way of my own; through the chief doctor's private apartments; and he's kind enough to keep two pistols in his drawer. I may be recaptured; but I shan't be hanged. I may be recaptured; but I particularly don't want your young friend to be captured at all. He's got his life before him; I don't choose he should suffer as I've suffered. I like the look of him; I like the way he turned all your medical tomfoolery upside down. So you'll understand I am at present wielding the power of a perfectly irresponsible sultan. I shall merely be rounding off a very pleasant holiday by blowing both your brains out, unless you will sit quite still and allow your young friend to tie you up with the ropes. That will give us a good start for our escape."

How he passed through the topsy-turvey transformation scene that followed Gale could afterwards barely remember; it seemed like a sort of dream pantomime, but its results were solid enough. Ten minutes later he and his strange deliverer were walking free in the woods beyond the last hedge of the garden, leaving the two medical gentlemen behind them in the arbour, tied up like two sacks of potatoes.

For Gabriel Gale the wood in which he walked was a new world of wonders. Every tree was a Christmas tree bearing gifts; and every gap in the woods was like a glimpse through the curtain for a child with a toy theatre. For a few moments before all these things had nearly disappeared in the darkness of something worse than death; till heaven had sent him a guardian angel in the shape of an escaped lunatic.

Gale was very young and his youth had not then found its vent and vocation by falling in love. There was in him something of those young Crusaders who made wild vows not to cut their hair till they found the Holy City. His liberty was looking and longing for something to bind itself; and at this moment he could think of but one thing in the world.

Two hundred yards along the path by the river he halted and spoke to his companion:

"It is you who have given me all this," he said. "Under God, and so far as my life goes, it is you who have created heaven and earth. You set up along my triumphal way these trees like seven-branched candlesticks with their grey branches silver in the sun. You spread before my feet these red leaves that are better than roses. You shaped clouds. You invented birds. Do you think I could enjoy all these things when I knew you were back again in the hell that you hate? I should feel I had tricked you out of everything you have given me. I should feel like a thief who had stolen the stars. You shan't go back there if I can help it; you saved me and I am going to save you. I owe you my life and I give it you; I vow I will share anything you suffer; God do so to me and more also, if aught but death part thee and me."

Thus were spoken in that wild place the wild words that determined the life of Gabriel Gale for so many years afterwards; and the walk that began in that wood turned into a wandering over the whole country by those two fantastic outlaws. As a matter of fact a sort of armed truce fell between them and their enemies, for each had something to fear from the other. Gale did not use all he discovered against the two doctors lest they should press the pursuit of his friend; and they did not press it lest he should retaliate with his own revelations. Thus the two came to roam practically unmolested until the day of that adventure, already described in the beginning of all these things, when he fell in love, and his crazy companion fell into a paroxysm which went very near to murder.

In every sense that dreadful day had changed all. That murderous outbreak had at last convinced a sadder and wiser Gabriel that he had other responsibilities besides those of his chivalric vow to his companion-in-arms; and he concluded that their companionship could only be rightly continued in some safe and more secluded form. Then it was that he put his friend into the comfortable and secret house in Cornwall, and spent most of his own time there, leaving a trustworthy servant on guard during his brief absences. His companion, whose name was James Hurrel, had been a business man of great ability and even audacity, until his schemes grew a little too big for his brain; and he lived happily enough in Cornwall, covering the tables with prospectuses and the walls with posters relative to various financial enterprises of the most promising kind. There he died, to all appearance equally happily; and Gale walked back from his funeral a free man.

Next morning, after a few hours' walking a rise and change in the rolling and wooded country told him that he was on the borders of his enchanted ground. He remembered something in the grouping of the trees, and how they seemed to huddle and stand on tiptoe with their backs to him, looking into the happy valley. He came to where the road curved over the hill, as he had come with his friend in former times; and saw below him the meadows falling steeply as thatched roofs and flattening out till they reached the wide and shallow river, and the ford and the dark inn called the Rising Sun.

The gloomy innkeeper of old days was gone, having found it less gloomy to take service in some stables in the neighbourhood; and a brisker individual with the look of a groom was the recipient of Gale's expansive praises of the beauty of the scene. Gale was good enough to inform the innkeeper of the beauty of the skies in the neighbourhood of his own inn, telling how he, Gale, had once seen a sunset in that valley quite peculiar to it and unequalled anywhere in the world; and how even the storm that had followed the sunset had been something very sublime in that style. His generalizations however were somewhat checked and diverted by a note which the innkeeper put into his hand, a note from the great house across the river. It was without any formal opening, as if the writer had hesitated about a form of address; and it ran:

"I want to hear the story and hope you will come over tomorrow (Thursday). I fear I shall be out today, as I have to go to see a Dr Wilson in Wimbledon about some work I have a chance of doing. I suppose you know we are pretty hard up in these days. DW."

The whole landscape seemed to him to darken for an instant as he read the letter, but he did not lose his brisk demeanour and breezy mode of speech.

"I find I made a mistake," he said, putting the note in his pocket, "and I must leave here almost at once. I have to visit another spot, if possible more picturesque and poetical than this one. It is Wimbledon that has skies of a strange and unique character at the present time. The sunsets of Wimbledon are famous throughout the world. A storm in Wimbledon would be an apocalypse. But I hope I shall come back here again sooner or later. Goodbye."

The proceedings of Mr Gale after this were rather more calculated and peculiar. First he sat on a stile and frowned heavily as if thinking hard. Then he sent off a telegram to a certain Dr Garth, who was a friend of his, and one or two other telegrams to persons in rather responsible positions. When he got to London he went into the offices of the vulgarest and most sensational newspaper he knew, and looked up the back files for the details of forgotten crimes. When he got to Wimbledon he had a long interview with a local house agent and ended up towards evening, outside a high garden wall with a green door, in a wide but empty and silent suburban road. He went quietly up to the door and barely touched it with his finger, as if seeing if the paint were wet. But the door, which was barred across with bands of decorative metal work and had every appearance of being shut, immediately fell ajar, showing the patchy colours of garden beds within. "I thought so," said Gale to himself and slipped into the garden, leaving the door ajar behind him.

The suburban family which he was presumably visiting, and with which the impoverished Diana Westermaine was presumably to take some post as governess or secretary, was evidently the sort who combined a new neatness with a certain early Victorian comfort and indifference to cost. The conservatories were of antiquated pattern, but full of rich and exotic things; there were things still more old-fashioned, such as a grey and rather featureless classical statue in the centre. Within a few yards of it were things so Victorian as croquet hoops and croquet mallets, as if a game had been in progress, and beyond it under the tree was a table set out with tea things, for people for whom tea was not a trifle. All these human things, unused at the moment by human beings, seemed to emphasize the emptiness of the garden. Or rather, so far as he was concerned, they emphasized the fact that it was almost empty, save for the one thing that could so strangely fill it with life. For far away down one of the paths pointing towards the kitchen garden he saw a figure moving as yet unconsciously towards him. It came out under an arch crowned with creepers and there, after so many years, they met. There seemed something symbolical of seriousness and crisis in the accident that they were both in black.

He had always been able to call up the memory of her dark vivid eyebrows and the high-tinted distinction of her face in connexion with corners of the blue dress she had worn; but when he saw her again he wondered that the face had not always annihilated all its lesser associations. She looked at him for a moment with bright motionless eyes and then said: "Well, really. You seem to be a rather impatient person."

"Possibly," he replied; "and yet I have waited four years."

"They are coming out to tea in a moment," she said somewhat awkwardly. "I suppose I must introduce you to them. I only accepted the post this morning; but they asked me to stay. I was going to wire to you."

"Thank God I followed you," he answered. "I doubt if the wire would have reached me – from this house."

"What do you mean?" she asked, "and how did you follow?"

"I did not like your Wimbledon address," he said: and with that, strange figures began to fill the garden, and she walked across to the tea table. Her face was somewhat paler and more severe than it used to be, but in her grey eyes there was a light not altogether extinguished, curiosity still shot with defiance. By the time they reached the table two or three people had collected round it; and the somewhat irregular visitor had saluted them in a regular and even punctilious fashion.

The host or hostess had apparently not yet become visible; there were only three gentlemen, presumably guests and perhaps members of a house-party. One was introduced as Mr Wolmer, a young man with a fair moustache and a tall fine figure that made his head look small; with a fine bridged nose that ought to have been like a hawk's if the prominence of the eyes and some deficiency of the chin had not somehow made it more like a parrot's. The second was a Major Bruce, a very short man with a very long head streaked with iron-grey hair, and an expression which suggested, truly enough, that he very seldom opened his mouth. The third was an elderly person with a black skull-cap on his bald head and a fringe or fan of red beard or whiskers; he was evidently a person of some importance and known as Professor Patterson.

Gale partook of tea and indulged in polite conversation in quite an animated fashion, wondering all the time who it was who ought to have been at the head of the table, where Diana Westermain was pouring out the tea. The demeanour of the man named Wolmer was rather restless; and in a little while he stood up and began, as if from the necessity of doing something, to knock the croquet balls about on the lawn. Gale, who was watching him with some interest, followed suit by picking up a mallet and trying some particular trick of putting two balls through a hoop. It was a trick which needed a test of some minuteness, for he went down on his hands and knees to examine the position more closely.

"Going to put your head through the hoop?" asked Wolmer rudely; for he had been growing more and more impatient, almost as if he had taken a mysterious dislike to the newcomer.

"Not quite," answered Gale good-humouredly as he rolled the balls away. "Uncomfortable position, I should think. Like being guillotined."

Wolmer was glaring balefully at the hoop and said something in a thick voice that sounded like "Serve you right." Then he suddenly whirled his mallet above his head like a battle-axe and brought it down with a crash on the hoop, driving it deep into the turf. There was something indescribably shocking about the pantomime, following instantly on the image that had just been suggested of a human head in the hoop. They felt as if an act of decapitation had been done before their very eyes.

"Better put down that mallet now," said the professor in a soothing voice, putting a rather shaky hand on the other's arm.

"Oh, I'll put it down then," said Wolmer, and slung it away over his shoulder like a man putting the hammer at the Highland Sports. It flew through the air like a thunderbolt, striking the forlorn plaster statue in the centre and breaking it off short at the top. Mr Wolmer laughed in a rather uncontrolled fashion; and then strode away into the house.

The girl had been watching these things with her dark brows bent and her pallor growing somewhat more marked. There was an unpleasant silence, and then Major Bruce spoke for the first time.

"It's the atmosphere of this place," he said. "It is not very wholesome."

The atmosphere of the suburban garden as a matter of fact was very clear, sunny and pleasant, and Diana looked round with a growing and even creeping mystification at the gay flowerpots and the lawns golden in the evening light.

"Perhaps it is my own misfortune," resumed the Major reflectively. "The truth is there is something serious the matter with me. I have a malady which makes this particular place rather awful."

"What do you mean?" she asked quickly.

There was a short silence and then he answered stolidly.

"I am sane."

Then she looked once more at the warm sunshiny garden and began to shudder as if with cold. A thousand things came back to her out of the last few hours. She knew why she had dimly distrusted her new home. She knew now that there is only one place in the world where men say that they are sane.

As the little man with the long head walked away as stiffly as a wooden automaton, she looked round for Gale and found he had vanished. An appalling emptiness, a vast vacuum of terror, opened around her on every side. In that moment she had admitted many things to herself that had been but half conscious: and no one on earth mattered but the man who had vanished into a void. For the moment she balanced the possibility that she was really mad against the possibility that nobody else was sane; when she caught sight, through the gap of a hedge, of figures moving at the other end of the garden. The old professor in the skull-cap was moving rapidly but with trepidation, as if running on tiptoe, his long lean hands flapping like fins and his red chin-beard wagging in the wind. And behind him following, equally softly and swiftly, at the distance of a few yards, was the long grey figure of Gabriel Gale. She could fit together no fancy about what it all meant; she could only continue to stare across the flower-beds at the glass houses full of monstrous flowers, and be vaguely conscious of a sort of symbol in the headless statue in the centre; the god of that garden of unreason.

The next moment she saw Gale reappear at the other extremity of the long hedge and come towards her smiling in the sunshine. He stopped when he saw her white face.

"Do you know what this place is?" she whispered. "It is a madhouse."

"It's a very easy one to escape from," said Gale in a serene manner. "I've just seen the professor escape from it. He escapes regularly; probably on Wednesdays and Saturdays."

"This is no time for your jokes," she cried. "I tell you we've been trapped inside a madhouse."

"And I tell you we shall soon be outside the madhouse," he replied firmly. "And under those circumstances, I don't mind telling you that I regret to say it is not a madhouse."

"What do you mean?"

"It is something worse," replied Gale.

"Tell me what you mean," she repeated. "Tell me what you know about this horrible place."

"For me it will always be a holy place," he said. "Was it not under that arch there that you appeared out of the abyss of memory? And after all, it's a beautiful garden and I'm almost sorry to leave it. The house, too, makes a romantic background; and really we might be very comfortable here – if only it were a madhouse." And he sighed with regret.

Then after a pause he added, "I might say all I want to say to you in a nice, friendly, comfortable lunatic asylum – but not in a place like this. There are practical things to be done now; and here come the people who will do them!"

She was never able to fit together again the fragments of that bad dream and its wilder way of breaking up. To her astonishment she beheld a new group advancing up the garden path; in front was a red-haired man in a top hat, whose shrewd and good-humoured features were faintly familiar to her; behind were two stalwart figures, obviously in "plain clothes", and between them the unexpected apparition of Professor Patterson in handcuffs.

"Caught him setting fire to a house," said the red-haired man briefly. "Valuable documents."

Later in that bewildering stretch of hours, the friends seated themselves on a garden seat for explanations. "You remember Dr Garth, I think," said Gale to the lady. "He has been helping me to clear up this queer business. The truth is, the police have suspected the nature of this Wimbledon retreat for some time. No: it is not a lunatic asylum; it is a den of very accomplished professional criminals. They have hit on the ingenious idea of being certified as irresponsible by a medical confederate; so that the worst that can happen is that he may be censured for laxity in letting them escape. Look up the records, and you will find them responsible, or irresponsible, for quite a long catalogue of crimes. I happened to follow the notion up, because I happened to guess where the notion came from. By the way, I suppose this is the gentleman who engaged you as a typist."

As he spoke a small alert figure strode out of the house and across the lawns; his short beard thrust forward with something of the gesture of a terrier.

"Yes, that is Dr Wilson; I made arrangements with him only this morning," answered Diana, still staring.

The doctor came to a halt in front of them, turning his head right and left in the terrier fashion, and looking at them with wrinkled brows and lids.

"So this is Dr Wilson," said Gale politely. "Good day, Dr Starkey."

Then as the plain-clothes man shifted and closed round the doctor, Gale added reflectively:

"I knew you would never fail to take a hint."

A street or two away from the strange madhouse there was a sort of toy park, not much bigger than a back garden, but laid out in ornamental paths and planted with flowering shrubs, as an oasis for nomadic nurses trailing about the babies of that suburb. It was also ornamented with long seats with curly backs, and one of these seats in its turn was ornamented by a couple clad in black and endeavouring, with some bewilderment, to appear respectable. Wild as were the events of that afternoon, they had moved very rapidly and it was barely evening. The sunset was settling down about the corners of the sky and of the quaint little public garden, and there was little noise except the shrill but faint calling of some children lingering over some long-drawn-out game.

It was here that he told her the whole story of the rash vow and all that happened between the rescue in the riverside garden and the funeral in the Cornish churchyard.

"The only thing I don't understand," she said at last, "is why you thought they had got me to that place; or why you thought there was any such place."

"Why, because," he said, looking at the gravel path with a slight embarrassment, "because I really was not bragging when

I told Starkey at the beginning that I understood the sort of mind he had, and could exaggerate it in the way it was going. Starkey never missed a chance of applying or misapplying an idea, especially anybody else's idea. When poor Jimmy Hurrel boasted of being free from punishment because he was an escaped lunatic, I was sure that a seed had been sown in Starkey's mind that would sprout. I was sure he would follow it up and use it, as he used my fancy for the swing or the arbour. While Jim was alive he knew I had a motive for silence; but the moment Jim died he struck. He was very quick; his mind is like a flash of lightning; quick but crooked. He sent one of his chartered maniacs to brain me with a stone on my way to you. He intercepted my telegram, and lured you away before you could be told the whole story. But what I want to know is what you think of the whole story."

"The vow was certainly rash enough," she said. "All that time you might have been painting pictures and doing all sorts of good. It doesn't seem right that a genius should be tied to a lunatic by a few words."

He sat up very suddenly. "For God's sake don't say that!" he cried. "Don't say one oughtn't to tie oneself to a lunatic by a few words! Don't say that's wrong, I implore you, whatever else you say! A shocking thought! A perfectly foul idea!"

"What do you mean?" she asked. "Why not?"

"Because," he said, "I want you to make a rash vow. I want you to tie yourself with a few words to a lunatic."

There was a silence, at the end of which she smiled suddenly and put her hand on his arm.

"No," she said, "only a silly... I always liked you, even when I thought you really were a lunatic; that day when you stood on your head. But now I don't think my vow will be so very rash... What on earth are you doing now?... Oh, I say – for heaven's sake..."

"What else should I do," he answered calmly, "after what you have just said? I'm going to stand on my head again."

The children in the corner garden gazed with interest at a gentleman in funeral full-dress behaving in a somewhat unusual manner.

G K Chesterton

The Ball and the Cross

Evan MacIan is a passionate and fiery young Catholic. He is outraged one day by an editorial he reads in *The Atheist* and vents his anger by smashing the window of the paper's office. He then challenges the editor, Turnbull, to a duel.

The feuding men are thwarted at every turn in their attempt to find a suitable place for their fight. While the search goes on they continue their theological debate. They eventually arrive at a position of acceptance and mutual understanding before the story reaches its powerful conclusion.

The Man Who Knew Too Much

Horne Fisher is the man who knew too much. He has a brilliant mind and powers of deduction – but he always faces a moral dilemma. These eight adventures will amaze and delight as we follow Horne and his friend, Harold March, in the world of crime among eminent people.

G K Chesterton

The Man Who Was Thursday

Lucian Gregory and Gabriel Syme both dress as poets. In this disturbing fantasy, one is an Anarchist and the other is a policeman. In the surreal anarchist world they inhabit, one of them is voted onto the Anarchists' Council of Days and becomes 'Thursday'.

The Nightmare has just begun...

The Napoleon of Notting Hill

Picture a London in the future where democracy is dead. A little government minister is made King. The boroughs are suddenly declared separate kingdoms with their own city guard, banner and gathering cry, and the capital is plunged into a strange type of medieval warfare.

Then Notting Hill declares its independence...

G K Chesterton

The Paradoxes of Mr Pond

Mr Pond was a small, neat civil servant. There was nothing remarkable about him at all – except a pointed beard. However, he tells the most fascinating stories and has the most unorthodox way of solving crimes and mysteries.

These eight short stories include the extraordinary 'The Three Horsemen of the Apocalypse' about a Marshal's plans that go tragically wrong because, paradoxically, his soldiers obey him.

The Return of Don Quixote

Michael Herne is a gentle, unassuming librarian. When he is asked to play a king in a medieval play he reluctantly agrees. After the play is over, however, strange things begin to happen. Michael refuses to change back into his everyday clothes and other actors find it impossible to return to their real character. Set in the early 20th Century, this is the intriguing story of the rise of a new Don Quixote who introduces a medieval government into the world of big business.